J FICTION FUS

Fussell, Sandy.

Owl ninja

**Please check all items for damages
before leaving the Library.
Thereafter you will be held
responsible for all injuries
to items beyond reasonable wear.**

SAMURAI KIDS

OWL NINJA

SAMURAI KIDS

OWL NINJA

SANDY FUSSELL

CANDLEWICK PRESS

J
FICTION
FUS

This is a work of fiction. Names, characters, places, and incidents are either products of the author's imagination or, if real, are used fictitiously.

Text copyright © 2011 by Sandy Fussell
Illustrations copyright © 2011 by Rhian Nest James

First U.S. edition 2011

Library of Congress Cataloging-in-Publication Data is available.

Library of Congress Catalog Card Number pending

ISBN 978-0-7636-5003-2

10 11 12 13 14 15 BVG 10 9 8 7 6 5 4 3 2 1

Printed in Berryville, VA, U.S.A.

This book was typeset in Garamond Three.

Candlewick Press
99 Dover Street
Somerville, Massachusetts 02144

visit us at www.candlewick.com

THE SAMURAI KIDS

KYOKO A white-haired girl with pink eyes and extra fingers and toes. Her spirit is the Snow Monkey.

MIKKO A one-armed boy. His spirit is the Striped Gecko.

NIYA The one-legged boy who narrates the story. His spirit is the White Crane.

YOSHI A huge, strong boy who doesn't want to fight. His spirit is the Tiger.

TAJI A blind boy. His spirit is the Golden Bat.

NEZUME The last boy to join the Cockroach Ryu. His spirit is the Long-Tailed Rat.

THE TEACHER

SENSEI Also known as Ki-Yaga the wizard. He
was once a famous samurai warrior.

CONTENTS

CHAPTER ONE

真

DRUMBEAT

"Someone's coming!" Taji yells.

I reach Taji first. Not because I'm the fastest. I'm good at many things, but running isn't one of them. It's hard to sprint with just one leg. I get there fast because I'm practicing sword thrusts only a hop away.

I peer into the valley and see a short, stocky figure making his way up the mountain path.

"Who is it?" Kyoko flops onto the grass.

Mikko, Nezume, and Yoshi arrive, pushing and shoving one another out of the way. Like an upended bowl of rice noodles, they land in a tangled mess beside me.

I've got really good eyes because in my heart I am the White Crane, able to spot a beetle on the ground from the air. My sight takes wing, soaring deep into the valley. But I don't know how Taji does it. How can a blind kid see at all? When I asked him, he laughed at me. "You have to listen, Niya. You are much too noisy to see with your ears."

It's true. I like to laugh and jump and yell. *Aeeeyagh! Aeeeyagh!* When I am practicing, the White Crane screeches out across the *ryu*. Even when I'm sleeping, Mikko has to poke me in the ribs because I snore louder than a pondful of frogs.

"It's Master Onaku," I announce.

"Why is the swordsmith coming?" Yoshi voices the question we all want to ask.

Master Onaku is Sensei Ki-Yaga's oldest friend, and it's always a special occasion when he visits. We usually spend days preparing the food. Sensei says a samurai kid must be able to wield his sword on the battlefield and a sharp knife in the kitchen. But we don't fall for that. The cooking isn't really about training. It's about Onaku's big, round stomach. The Sword Master loves to eat.

Last time, we prepared fish soup, three-egg omelette, and honey rice pudding, the finest dessert in all of Japan. My nose follows the imaginary smell as it curls into a smoke ring and drifts skyward.

"We should tell Sensei," says Nezume.

Puff. The smell disappears, but my mouth is still watering.

"I'll go," I volunteer. Maybe our teacher is in the kitchen.

But I can't even get up onto my foot before Sensei's voice meets me. "Tell Master Onaku I am waiting in the tearoom."

Sensei always handles important business there. My friends and I don't like the tea ceremony. Too many rules.

Most days, Ki-Yaga slurps his pudding and sucks the splatters from his long white beard, but during the tea ceremony, he doesn't make a sound and he doesn't spill a drop.

By the time Onaku is almost to the top of the mountain, we have made up many stories to explain his visit.

"He's bringing us extra swords," suggests Mikko.

Not likely. Last year, at our Coming-of-Age Ceremony, we were given new swords—the long *katana* and the short *wakizashi,* dual weapons of the warrior samurai. Onaku is a master craftsman. One of his swords would last two lifetimes, so it can't be that.

Kyoko looks concerned. "Maybe Mrs. Onaku is sick." Sensei is a great healer, and Onaku wouldn't trust anyone else to care for his wife. We hope that's not the reason.

"Perhaps he has run out of wine," says Yoshi.

It's the most likely explanation of all. Sensei's *dokudami* wine smells like rotten fish, but Onaku would walk up the mountain and back at the promise of a bottle.

"Hello, young Cockroaches," he calls as he draws closer. "How goes the studying and the practicing? And how is Niya's nose?"

It's an old joke. When I first came to the Cockroach

Ryu, I fell over many times during training. Twice I broke my nose. Then twice more Taji caught me unaware with the flat blade of his wooden practice sword and broke it for me.

"Our master is waiting in the tearoom," says Yoshi.

Onaku nods and hurries off to find Sensei. Something is wrong. Usually, the Sword Master will chat and joke for hours, telling us stories of the days when he was a boy listening at Ki-Yaga's feet. Sensei was old, even then.

Across the valley, a drumbeat echoes. *Thum. Thum.*

"What's that?" Nezume asks.

Ta-thum. Ta-thum. Thum.

Yoshi shakes his head. We all do. No one knows what it means, but we don't like it. It kicks hard against my chest and makes me nervous.

Yoshi puts his finger to his lips and gestures for us to follow. Yoshi is our leader, and I'd follow him anywhere. He has the spirit of a tiger — big and strong. When an earthquake rolled me off the mountain, he climbed through the darkness to my rescue.

Yoshi pads noiselessly to the tearoom. Crouching low behind Sensei's row of potted bonsai trees, he places his ear against the wall. We copy him, one by one. The wall is made of thin rice paper, so it's easy to hear every word.

"You were right, Ki-Yaga," Onaku says with a sigh. "It has happened just as you said it would."

I can see his blurred shadow, head bowed and shoulders slumped. Onaku looks old and beaten. The Sword Master is strong, and his spirit is tougher than twice-folded steel. What could make him clutch his head in his hands?

"Yes. Sometimes I really wish to be wrong." Sensei sounds sad. He places his arm around his friend.

Uneasiness surrounds us all. Things that were once solid are now wavering, hard to grasp. It's worse than when the mountain trembles, but that same air of foreboding hangs low over our heads.

I look at Yoshi, who shrugs. Yoshi looks at Kyoko, and she looks at Taji and Nezume. Mikko shakes his head. We haven't got a clue what's happening, but I know in my stomach that it's not good. Misery binds our worried faces together.

Even when a samurai is unhappy, he should never lower his guard. He'll be even more miserable if he's surprised by an enemy sword.

The door slides open, and we're caught by the
razor swipe of Sensei's steely gaze.

The door slides open, and we're caught by the razor swipe of Sensei's steely gaze. Our faces glow red and pink like the setting sun.

"Your walls have many ears, Ki-Yaga," Onaku says.

Sensei's face is like my calligraphy homework: impossible to read. "What have you heard?" he asks.

"Everything," Yoshi mumbles.

We look at the ground, hiding our sunset faces.

Yoshi scuffs his sandals in the dirt. "It was my idea. I'm responsible."

"Excellent." Sensei claps his hands. "A samurai must be a good listener. It gives him an edge even sharper than his sword. Now, Niya, how should a samurai listen?"

Our teacher always asks me the hardest questions. He says my brain needs more exercise than my leg. But I know this one because Taji taught me earlier.

"A samurai should listen with his eyes and see with his ears."

Sensei grins. First at me, then Taji. Finally, his smile collects us all. He's pleased because we are working together.

Last year, our team won the Samurai Trainee Games.

Before that, everyone laughed at us. Mikko with his one arm; blind Taji; Yoshi, who refused to fight. Me with my one leg and Nezume, who ran away from the cruel Dragon Master to live like an animal in the forest. They laughed at Kyoko most of all. "Freak girl," they jeered, pointing at her white hair, pink eyes, and six fingers and toes.

They stopped laughing when we won. We were no longer the students no other school wanted; we were the samurai kids everyone wanted to be. We made a lot of new friends. Except from the Dragon Ryu. It's hard to shake hands with your opponents when they have already gone home.

"What's happening?" asks Kyoko. "What does the drum mean?"

"Things I hoped you would never hear, Little Cockroaches," Sensei says. "For ten days, the drum will call the mountain *ryu*s to war. When it stops, the fifty-year peace will be over. The *ryu*s must pledge their allegiance to the Lord of the North or the Lord of the South. In times of war, a samurai must serve with his sword."

My stomach hurts, and the White Crane frantically batters its wings against my heart. The *ryu*s will fight on different sides.

I think of the Eagle Ryu. And the Rabbit. And all the others we competed against at the Samurai Trainee Games. The Games are real now.

Thum. Thum. Ta-thum.

The drum kicks even harder into my chest, and it hurts to breathe.

Will friends now be forced to fight as enemies?

CHAPTER TWO

仁

BEWARE THE
DRAGON

"I won't fight." Yoshi plants his feet like the roots of a giant cherry tree. It would take an enormous wind to shift even one of his sandals.

"You don't have to." Sensei's words blow gently. The tree falls with a thud as Yoshi crumples, relieved, onto the grass.

We understand why our friend doesn't fight. It's not about strength or bravery. Yoshi is stronger than the rest of us pulling together. He carries a great weight around every day. When he was only seven, he threw his opponent from the wrestling ring. The boy hit his head on a rock and died.

"The drum is not calling to *us*," Sensei says. "The Cockroach Ryu isn't going into battle. We are not bound to any lord. My days of service were completed long ago."

The other *ryu*s belong to a *daimyo,* a lord they defend in times of trouble and war. In return, the *daimyo* looks after his samurai and their students. With its dilapidated buildings and old equipment, it's obvious our *ryu* has no lord to pay for its upkeep.

We have always been poor. But we are rich in honor. Once Sensei was the Emperor's personal bodyguard, teaching swordsmanship to the royal children. The Son of Heaven himself rewarded Ki-Yaga by releasing him from service. Now Sensei answers to no *daimyo,* not even the Emperor.

"I didn't want to fight either." Kyoko stretches her slender arms around Yoshi's broad shoulders. There's only one thing in the world that feels better than a stomach full of honey pudding, and that's a hug from Kyoko.

We all pile on top of her and Yoshi, to show our support, and poke and prod each other in the ribs.

"Get your foot out of my mouth," Mikko mumbles at me.

"What did you say?" I pretend I don't understand.

Aaargh. Nezume yelps and groans from somewhere underneath.

"If you don't move your bony elbow out of my ear, I'll chop if off. Then you won't have *any* arms," Taji threatens Mikko.

With a great roar, Yoshi shakes us all apart.

"See how dedicated my students are," Sensei says to Onaku. "Even now they do wrestling practice."

"I think they need a lot more." The Sword Master

We all pile on top of her and Yoshi.

smiles wider than the green tree frog we found swimming in Sensei's *dokudami* wine last week.

Everyone laughs. Except Kyoko. She's not even smiling.

"Someone pulled my hair," she complains, flicking the ice-white strands out of her eyes. "It took me forever to get it rolled into place. Look at this mess."

Samurai kids always wear their hair twisted into a topknot, pinned tight. But now Kyoko's hair swirls in a fall of snow, to hang like mist around her shoulders. "Who did it?" she demands.

I'm not stupid. I keep my mouth shut. Kyoko's hair might be soft and silky, but her fists are hard as rock. And when she kicks, her six toenails scrape like splinters of bamboo. I've already got a scar to prove it.

"One day this samurai girl will do great damage in the hearts of men. More than any of my swords ever did," says Onaku.

Kyoko hides her face in her hands, but I can see her smile shining through.

Ta-thum. Thum. Thump.

The drum doesn't frighten me anymore. It drifts over our heads, through the valley, to the next mountain peak. In my heart, the White Crane sleeps peacefully. It doesn't even raise its head to listen. I pull my jacket tight around my ears. It's autumn in the mountains, and when the sun moves down into the valley, the air grows cold with the promise of snow.

"Why do we keep training if we're never going to fight?" Mikko brandishes an imaginary weapon, finishing with a lethal thrust through Yoshi's chest.

Grrr. Yoshi growls a warning, and the pretend sword is quickly returned to its scabbard.

"What use are swords if we can't wield them in battle?" grumbles Mikko.

"Would you like to teach my students this lesson?" Sensei bows low to show his respect for Master Onaku.

Some men pay a year's wages for one of Onaku's weapons. They travel for weeks, then wait for days while the Sword Master creates the perfect blade for each hand.

A samurai's sword is his most treasured possession. He wears it on his belt, but it is always close to his heart and it sings into his soul. My sword shines bright and sings loud enough for Onaku to hear. Even now, when it should be listening politely.

"May I borrow your weapon, Niya?" Onaku asks. "I need to make a point."

We're all paying close attention now. *The point of a sword is very sharp,* as Sensei says.

Carefully, I draw the blade and pass it to the Sword Master. I keep the cutting edge inward because if I tip over and fall, Onaku might be killed.

"It is bad manners to face the blade outward," Sensei taught us. "It is even worse manners to slice a friend in two."

Onaku holds my weapon flat across both his palms. "My swords are not forged to carve sinew and muscle. They are not kitchen knives. See? A samurai sword is an object of beauty and honor, not a butcher's tool."

With the cutting edge facing his stomach, he returns the sword to me. "May blood never touch this blade."

I agree. Especially if it's my blood. I cautiously place my sword back in its scabbard.

"Look with your ears and you will see the blade sing," Sensei reminds us.

"That's not hard," says Taji. "Niya's sword is almost as noisy as he is."

"I've got a lot to say," I protest, poking out my tongue. "Mikko's loud, too. Sometimes I have to yell over the top of him."

Now Mikko pokes out his tongue. "But when you yell, Niya, even the trees tremble. You're noisy *and* dangerous."

I grin at the compliment. If an enemy hears me coming, he'll just run away.

Our life has always had a pattern of comfortable sameness. Breakfast and practice. Lunch and study. And after dinner, "More practice!" Sensei calls every hour until bed.

Only very old men can remember wartime. And only even older men, like Sensei, know what it was like to fight.

"What about Sensei's sword?" Nezume asks. "He carried it into many battles. It must have been covered with blood."

"People say he wielded the fastest sword in all of Japan. Sometimes his opponent could not even see the blade," Taji adds.

Onaku grins and winks. "Perhaps they could not see it because it was not there."

That can't be true. Not even Ki-Yaga would go into battle without a sword.

But Sensei is grinning, too. "Sometimes I think my students are deaf. Or they have memories like fishing nets. What is the most important thing I have taught you?" he asks us.

It's an easy question, and we don't have to think about the answer. It was one of the first lessons we learned.

"A true samurai doesn't need a sword," says Yoshi.

Sensei nods. "I am a good swordsman, but I am an even better teacher. I can teach the deaf to hear and the forgetful to tie knots in their nets."

Could it be true? Did Sensei fight swordless? The villagers say he is a wizard. They say some nights he turns into a *tengu* mountain goblin and they see his black crow shadow fly across the moon. My friends don't believe a word of it, but sometimes Sensei speaks inside my head, so I'm not as sure.

"What's that smell?" Onaku asks, wrinkling his nose.

It's hard to imagine any odor offending the Sword

Master. When he swigs Sensei's fishy wine, he doesn't even hold his nostrils closed. But Taji is the expert when it comes to smells. Without eyes, he finds other ways to see. And his nose never misses a sniff.

"It's Niya's slipper," he says with a laugh. "He trod in horse dung when he fed Uma this morning."

Mikko pulls my slipper off my foot and waves it in Kyoko's face.

"Yuck," she squeals.

"I washed it. Give it back." If I had another one, I'd throw it at him.

Sensei takes off one of his own slippers and hands it to me. He tucks his other foot behind him and smiles.

I am like you, the wizard whispers inside my head. *I do not care if I have only one slipper.*

The game is over, and Sensei is still looking at me, his bright eyes drilling deep. He has another lesson for me to find.

Ta-thum. Ta-thum. Thump.

The drum leads me to it. We're not out of danger yet. The Dragon Master is looking forward to fighting us, and for him, the war is a convenient excuse. He has a score to settle.

"The Dragon Master won't like it when he finds out we're not going to war," I say miserably.

Sensei nods. "I do not believe blood must be spilled to solve a problem, but the Dragon Master thinks differently."

Taji shakes his head, confused. "Why would a teacher want to lead his students into war?"

"Why would he choose to risk their lives?" Kyoko is puzzled, too.

But Nezume understands the Dragon Master. "He doesn't care who he hurts. He sees glory in any victory, and he'll do whatever it takes for his side to win. Especially if he is given the chance to fight against us."

No one argues with that. Nezume would know. He studied at the Dragon Ryu for two years, and the Dragon Master's cruelty is written in the scars across his back.

"Dishonor and stupidity go together," Sensei says sadly. "The Dragon Master's brain is as empty as Niya's other slipper."

He means the one I haven't got.

"We have to do something. We can't stand back just because we don't have to fight. No one should have to. Not even the Dragons," insists Yoshi.

Sensei nods in agreement. "All war is about nothing important. When something is nothing, it is not worth fighting about."

Ki-Yaga is a Zen master. They're experts at Nothing. And I'm good at Zen, too. I think about nothing all the time.

Ta-thum. Thump. The drum dares us to make it stop.

"Only the Emperor or the Shogun can silence a war drum," Taji says.

"The Shogun is away in the far north, but the Emperor is in winter residence at Toyozawa Castle. We will go there and ask the Emperor, the Son of Heaven, to help. But we must be careful." Sensei frowns, his brow wrinkling like rice paper. "Not everyone will want to see this war end before the first sword stroke. The mountain lords will insist on the right to settle their differences with the sword."

"And the Dragon Master will do all he can to make certain the bloodshed begins," says Onaku. "He will see Ki-Yaga's peacemaking as an attempt to deprive the Dragon Ryu of its chance to win great honor and distinction."

We understand that. Beware the Dragon. But we're also excited to be going on a journey.

I can't wait to see the castle again. Many years ago, when I was too young for school, my father and mother took me to see the Emperor honor the great samurai warrior Mitsuka Manuyoto. Now Mitsuka lives as a hermit beside the ocean, but when he was a boy, he studied at the Cockroach Ryu and slept in my bed. His name is scratched into the wood above my pillow. I carved my name beneath it. His writing was as poor as mine.

I remember the castle. Food, singing, dancing, and music.

But the only music now is the drum.

Ta-thum. Thum. Thum.

Ten days to war.

"We leave at once, before the Dragon Master realizes what we are trying to do," Sensei announces. "We must ask the Emperor to move quickly."

But it might not be possible for him to move quickly. Our Emperor is even bigger and rounder than Onaku. Maybe he could sit on the Dragon Master. Imagining the Dragon Master squashed flat, I smile wider than the drunken tree frog.

Sensei's brilliant eyes search my face. *Is the wizard reading my mind?* I practice Zen thoughts and think of nothing. But it doesn't help. Sensei doesn't stop at nothing.

"Taji and Kyoko will pack food for the journey," Sensei instructs. "Yoshi, Mikko, and Nezume will gather clothes and weapons."

"I'll help with that," Onaku volunteers.

"Niya will go and catch Uma."

Once we would have drawn bamboo straws to see who had to go near his snarling teeth. That was before I discovered he liked honey rice pudding as much as I do. Now we're the best of friends. But we can't load our goods on his back, we'll have to carry everything ourselves. Uma is a proud warrior horse. He'll let us ride, but he won't cart raincoats and rice cakes. Not for all the pudding in Japan.

By the time the sun sinks low into the valley, we're packed and ready to leave. Sensei goes first, leading Uma through the dusk, down the path to the village. When

Yoshi and I walked this way alone, I saw shapes shifting in the darkness. Wolves. *Tanuki* dogs. But here with my friends and our ferocious horse, there is nothing to fear. Not even Grandfather's ghost stories could frighten me now.

Our spirits shine bright in the deepening gloom. Yoshi, the Tiger; Taji, the Golden Bat, who doesn't need eyes to see; Mikko, the Striped Gecko; Kyoko, the mischievous Snow Monkey; Nezume, the Long-Tailed Rat; and me. I am the White Crane, spreading my wings over them all, a cloak against the thump of the drum.

Night turns the trees gray and spectral. It's a four-hour journey to the village, but it will take longer traveling with Uma. The ground is uneven where last year's earthquake has refolded the path, and it's easy for a horse to stumble if we move too quickly.

I walk second from the end. Not because I'm slow—even with one leg I can travel as fast as the others—but because Onaku brings up the rear and I like to talk to him. I like to hear about the adventures he and Sensei had together.

"The Emperor will be pleased to see Ki-Yaga," I say.

"Maybe there will be a welcoming parade when the Son of Heaven hears we are coming."

Onaku lifts one eyebrow, then the other.

"The Emperor was so pleased with Sensei's service that he rewarded our teacher with his freedom," I continue. "He was the only royal bodyguard ever to receive such a great honor. Maybe there'll be fireworks."

Onaku grins, and his belly begins to jiggle as the laugh works its way to his face. "Is that what Sensei told you?"

"Well, not exactly. But I thought . . ."

Onaku's laugh erupts over my words. "I remember it a little differently. The Emperor yelled so loud that his words are still stamped inside my ear. His face went purple, and his eyes bulged bigger than a bubble-faced goldfish. 'If I ever see you around here again, Ki-Yaga, I'll chop off your head' was what he said. As I recall, Ki-Yaga and I left very quickly."

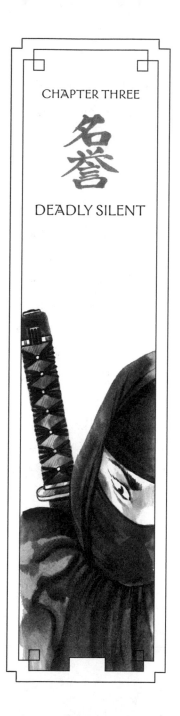

CHAPTER THREE

名誉

DEADLY SILENT

Half a moon lights our way forward, the drumbeat pushing against our backs. We keep going.

The path has narrowed now, forcing us to walk in single file. It's cold, but that's not why I'm shivering. Samurai kids wear many layers of clothing. I could walk through the snow and not feel a single icy drip. I'm worried about what might happen to Sensei when we reach the castle.

Even I can't yell louder than the rising night wind and the pounding drum, so I send my question down the path, echoing from friend to friend.

"Ask Sensei why the Emperor wants to chop off his head. Pass it on," I whisper to Nezume, walking in front of me.

"I'd like to know that, too. Sensei's head belongs where it is," Nezume says.

He repeats my question to Mikko.

Mikko tells Taji, and I just catch Mikko's muffled words. "Ask Sensei why the emperor wants to drop his head. Niya needs to know."

I never said that! But a whispered message has a life of its own, and like the bamboo snake, it sheds its skin and changes as it wriggles on. I hear Taji's voice. Then

Kyoko's. Finally, Yoshi's words bellow through the darkness. "Why does Niya want to know that?"

"Know what?" Sensei's voice rises to hang like a question mark.

The path has widened, and now we're close together again. I could have saved a lot of trouble and asked Sensei myself.

"Niya needs to know why the Emperor wants you to drop dead," Yoshi says.

It's not what I said at all. Still, it's near enough.

"Is it true, Sensei?" Kyoko is worried, but Sensei laughs.

"Yes. The Emperor was very angry. But there is a long line of men waiting to collect my head. Some, like the Dragon Master, would even push the Emperor out of the way to get it." Sensei laughs again. "But I have more important things to worry about. Yoshi's stomach is rumbling as loud as the war drum. There is a cave just below the next bend where we can eat and rest. I'll tell the story then."

Yoshi is much bigger than the rest of us, and he loves his food almost as much as the Sword Master does. We always tease him about it.

"Better get in quick." Mikko winks at Nezume. "Otherwise Master Onaku and Yoshi will eat everything. Rice-paper wrapping and all."

Cheeky Striped Gecko. The wrapping is meant to be eaten.

"I'm so hungry, I could eat a handful of lizards and maybe a long-tailed rat or two." Yoshi grins and bares his tiger teeth.

I'm hungry enough to eat a horse.

Uma snorts a warning in my direction. Now even the wizard's horse is inside my brain. I must be light-headed from lack of food. We didn't eat before we left, and the time for dinner has long passed.

"A samurai must learn to overlook the hunger in his gut and concentrate on his head. He cannot worry about food in the middle of battle," Sensei taught us. "And if he does, he may not have a head."

I have always been attached to my head, so I try to ignore my stomach.

The entrance to the cave is narrow, and inside, the space is smaller than the *ryu*'s tiny kitchen. But no one complains. We feel warm and safe, wedged tight. Even the sound of the drum is muffled into noiselessness. If only the beat didn't continue echoing its warning inside my head.

Mikko and Kyoko unpack egg rolls and noodle cakes. Yoshi passes the bowls, and Nezume places the water bottle in the center. Taji lights the tree-wax candles and holds the last one close in front of his face.

"What are you doing?" Nezume asks.

It's a good question. We need the candlelight, but it makes no difference to Taji. He's always in the dark.

"Can you see something?" Kyoko looks hopeful.

Long ago Onaku told us the story of an old blind villager. One morning he opened his eyes and the blindness was gone. Every night we wish for the same miracle for Taji, but every morning he is still blind. Sensei says it doesn't matter. Taji already sees better than the rest of us staring together.

"Sometimes I can see gray in the black." Taji moves the candle to-and-fro.

"Is that a good sign?" Kyoko asks Sensei.

She wants to know if it means Taji might see one day.

Sensei nods. "It is a very good sign. There is no black and white in the world. Only black and gray."

But I want Taji to see all the colors of our world, not just its shadows. I want to show him the pink and orange of the sun rising over the mountains. The bright white of Kyoko's hair. And the blue blazing in Sensei's eyes.

Our conversation fades into a quiet camaraderie of food and thought, until the silence is finally big enough to hold Sensei's story. He places his chopsticks across his bowl. His words grow large to fill the spaces between us, drawing us even closer to one another.

"Many years ago, before you were born, when even Onaku was a young man, I was the Emperor's body-guard. I taught swordsmanship and zazen meditation to the castle children. I protected the Emperor's life with my own."

Our legs are folded, but our backs are straight and proud. Once Sensei taught princes and princesses. Now he chooses to teach us.

"Assassins are masters of disguise. They sneak beneath the night. They hide in small spaces," Sensei says.

Like a ninja! I remember what my father told me about them. They are ancient enemies of the samurai. They kill in secret, their dishonorable deeds cloaked in darkness. They don't even carry proper swords. They're worse than the Dragons.

"Some assassins are very hard to see. The one that crept to murder the Emperor was almost not there. But I watched with my ears and killed him before he could strike."

"It was a ninja," I announce. "They're experts at hide-and-sneak. The ninja are without honor." I'm pleased I worked it out first. Sensei always says my brain is a good athlete. It doesn't need two legs to run.

But our teacher doesn't look impressed this time.

"The ninja are not enemies of the Cockroach Ryu. You mustn't judge too quickly, Niya. If you stick your foot in your mouth, you will fall flat on your face."

Chastened, I nod respectfully.

"The Emperor must have been very grateful. You saved his life," Mikko says, rescuing me from our teacher's frown.

Sensei shakes his head. "At first, the Emperor wished *himself* dead. The assassin was his youngest brother."

Kyoko gasps.

Sensei killed a member of the imperial family. The penalty for that crime is death. There's no excuse at all. Yet somehow Sensei is still alive.

Ki-Yaga is a wizard. I'm sure of it now. It's the only possible explanation.

We sit in stunned silence. We know what should have happened next. To avoid dishonor, a samurai must slice his stomach and spill its contents onto the bamboo matting. It is called *seppuku.* The practice is forbidden under the new laws, but Sensei is a samurai of the old ways and the Emperor would have expected this private show of respect.

But Sensei couldn't have sacrificed his stomach. No wonder the Emperor wants his head.

"The Emperor left my death sentence open until another time. Then he banished me from his presence. Onaku has already told you the end of the story."

Yoshi is quick to defend our teacher. "There was no dishonor in what you did."

"You had no face to save," I agree.

Sensei grins. "Only the contents of my last meal. Steamed fish and seaweed rice, I think. Do you remember, Onaku?"

The Sword Master nods, patting his belly. "It was very

tasty and worth keeping. You made the right decision, Ki-Yaga."

"Do you think the Emperor still wants to cut your head off?" Kyoko's face wrinkles with worry.

"One cannot be sure. Few debts are never collected," Sensei says with a shrug. "We have a long way to go before we find out. Come, Little Cockroaches."

He claps his hands and Nezume jumps, knocking some of his rice onto Yoshi's plate.

"Thanks," Yoshi says, between hurried extra mouthfuls.

My appetite is gone. I'm much too worried about Sensei to eat.

Taji and Kyoko pack up the leftover food as Onaku helps himself to the last egg roll.

The sound of the drum fades as we descend toward the valley, but the echo of it still blasts and batters inside my head. War is marching to the mountains, and if we fail to stop its advance, many of our friends will die.

It's very late by the time we reach Onaku's home at the edge of the village. Mrs. Onaku is waiting at the door.

"Quickly, inside," she says, looking beyond us into the darkness. "Strangers passed through the village this afternoon. We'll tether Uma inside the smithy."

A night surrounded by armor and swords is a dream come true for an old warrior horse. Uma bares his teeth in a wet, wide smile.

Onaku isn't worried by the falling spray of spittle. He has other things on his mind. "Is there anything to eat, good wife?"

"I have supper prepared," she replies, smiling. "But first I must look after these children. They are exhausted. Especially Niya."

"I'm all r-r-ight," I stutter and mumble, struggling to breathe.

Yoshi prods me in the ribs. My friends know what the problem is. Mrs. Onaku smells like cherry blossoms, and her voice runs like honey to clog my thoughts until I can't think at all. Whenever she speaks to me, the goldfish in my stomach flip and wriggle and my face goes bright red.

Fortunately, she never notices.

"I've put the boys in this room." She opens a screen door, delicately painted with samurai battle scenes. All the warriors on the wall have Onaku's face but none of them have his stomach. Mrs. Onaku is a skilled painter and a loving wife.

Onaku knows how lucky he is.

"I am no good at zazen," he told us. "When I close my eyes, her face fills my thoughts. Until there is no room for Nothing."

If I had a wife that looked like Mrs. Onaku, I'd never close my eyes.

"Kyoko can come with me," she says. "I'm sure she needs a break from your smelly boys, Ki-Yaga."

Mikko grunts and Taji makes a face. After wrestling practice, Kyoko smells as much as we do. Sometimes worse. Our Snow Monkey hates bathing in the icy waters of the *ryu* river.

"I'll bring supper in soon," Mrs. Onaku promises.

My mouth waters. She's a wonderful cook. No wonder Onaku has a big stomach.

"Where's Sensei?" Taji asks. Trust Taji to notice what we didn't see. Sensei and Onaku have slipped away.

"They have much to organize for tomorrow. And to

help, you should eat and get some sleep." Mrs. Onaku smiles, and I silently promise to eat and sleep forever.

Supper is honey rice cakes with plum juice. It's gone quickly, and I'm alone in the dark with my friends.

"Hey, Niya! Would you like Mrs. Onaku to tuck you in?" Mikko teases.

I throw a pillow at him and grin as the thwack finds his head.

"I'm worried," Nezume whispers into the darkness.

He always is. Like the long-tailed rat, his nose twitches and his eyes shine anxiously.

"Me too," admits Mikko. "What if we can't stop the war? What if Sensei dies trying?"

"There's nothing to be concerned about." Yoshi's voice is calm and authoritative. "Sensei's head wields more power than any sword stroke."

We already knew this, but we feel better now that Yoshi has reminded us.

Especially Nezume. "Thanks, Yosh," he says.

"Rise and shine, Little Cockroaches."

Blearily, I open my eyes. The only thing shining is Ki-Yaga's bamboo torch.

"It must be the middle of the night," Mikko moans.

"Five hours of sleep. The perfect amount." Sensei's voice booms in our ears.

Five is Sensei's favorite number. He teaches us about Godai—the five tiers of Zen. Earth, water, fire, wind, and sky. The most powerful of all is sky, where the White Crane and the black *tengu* take flight. But sky is also void. It's no surprise that Nothing should be so important.

We dress as quickly as we can. Underwear, trousers, jacket, kimono. Layer after layer tied together. It makes us look noble and proud, but it takes forever to put on. Not good for a quick getaway.

"Watch out!" Taji ducks as Mikko's *obi* sash flicks past and slaps me in the face.

"Why are we leaving now?" grumbles Nezume. "It's still dark."

"My tearoom walls are not the only ones with ears," Sensei says. "When the mountain lords hear that the Cockroach Ryu is empty, they will be suspicious. Each will think we have joined the forces of the other, and they will send spies to find out what we are planning."

"Will they send the Dragon Master?" Nezume asks nervously.

"As soon as he realizes we serve no lord, he will know what we intend to do. And he will quickly work out where we are going. He will follow us, but for his own purpose." Sensei frowns. "Some people would be happy if we disappeared on our way to the castle."

"We're not scared," Taji says.

"Definitely not," agrees Yoshi.

Nezume, Mikko, and I add our support. My face is brave, but inside my heart, the White Crane hides. It's not as brave as I'm pretending to be.

The Sword Master and his wife have risen, too. Kyoko is waiting with them, holding Sensei's favorite traveling staff, the one with the owl feathers tied at the top.

"I wish I could come with you," Onaku says. "I would like to see the castle again, and I have a package to deliver."

"We need you here, old friend. Who else could I trust with Uma? I will see that the Emperor gets his new sword."

The village streets are quiet and empty.
Darker than old cherrywood.

Onaku hands Sensei the package. Two sword handles protrude from the end. *If one is for the Emperor, then who gets the other?* The last time we carried a spare sword, we found Nezume in the forest and gave it to him. Now he's one of us. But this time, the second sword is too large for another samurai kid.

Mrs. Onaku grips her husband's arm tight. She knows we're heading into danger, but she trusts Sensei. We all do.

Sensei raises his hand to signal good-bye, and Onaku nods. The most important conversations between friends don't need words.

Sensei turns and strides quickly into the night. As usual, we hurry to keep up.

The village streets are quiet and empty. Darker than old cherrywood.

"Where is everyone?" Taji asks.

"Asleep in bed," Mikko mutters. "Where we should be."

Nezume sighs. "Even the drummer isn't awake yet."

"No. It's something deeper than that," says Taji. "The village is almost empty. Listen. There's nothing at all. Where are the snuffles and the sounds of sleep? It's too quiet."

"Sometimes it is what you don't hear that matters most," Sensei agrees.

Where did they all go? A whole village can't just disappear.

Sensei hears every question, even the ones I haven't asked yet. "Some have answered the drum and marched to war. Others have hidden far away."

Now we're quiet, too, thinking of the villagers who might never return if we fail.

Once the village was alive with noise.

Now it's dead silent.

CHAPTER FOUR

忠
誠

HELL VALLEY

Sensei leads us west, toward the castle. Beyond that stretches the ocean. Even in the early morning gloom, I know I've been this way before. This is the direction toward my home.

Many years ago Father and Grandfather brought me along the same path to the Cockroach Ryu.

"I am going to be a samurai warrior," I yelled up the mountain. The White Crane shrieked in echo.

Waving my crutches with pride, I puffed out my chest. "The great Ki-Yaga wants to teach me."

"I thought he was dead," Grandfather grumbled and wheezed. "He probably will be by the time we get there. I might beat him to it."

Sensei might be old, but he walks fast. We hurry behind him, pushing and shoving each other along. Giggling at Taji's silly voices. Laughing at Mikko's jokes. Samurai kids are not skilled at sneaking. We wouldn't make very good ninja at all.

At the fork in the path, Sensei turns left.

I try to keep my voice still, but the quake in my stomach rises to shake my words.

"Are we going into the Jigokudani Valley, Sensei?" I ask.

Now Nezume's worried, too. "What's wrong with the valley?"

"Nothing that bothers me," Sensei says.

But there's plenty for the rest of us to be nervous about. They don't call it Hell Valley for nothing. Boiling mud. Thick steam mists to get lost in. Great cracks in the ground to fall through. And most terrifying of all, the restless souls of the dead. If we die here, who will save the mountains from war?

Yoshi moves to walk beside me. "Your face has turned white."

Mikko thinks it's funny. "You look like you've seen a ghost, Niya."

I haven't yet. Ask me later. We'll be surrounded by them.

"My grandfather told me the valley is haunted by demons," I tell them. "Transparent shreds of flesh hang from their limbs. Their eyes burn like molten rock. They like to play tricks. And when they tell the future, it always comes true." My voice quivers and cracks.

"One day Niya will be a better storyteller than I am." Sensei places his arm around my shoulder. "Already he can frighten his friends with just a few words."

His praise lifts my spirit high, and the White Crane forgets its fear, soaring bravely into Hell Valley's gaping mouth.

"Since when did we care how people look? Do we worry about a missing arm? Or leg? Or slab of flesh?" Sensei plants his staff in the soft ground. "Dead people are usually very polite. They like to say hello and talk about the weather."

Mikko giggles and nudges Yoshi, but Sensei doesn't laugh. "Some ghosts play tricks because they get bored," he says. "Death is monotonous. But every spirit I've spoken to tells the truth. Their sense of honor is not dead, only their bodies."

"You talk to ghosts?" Kyoko's mouth drops open.

"All the time. I am very old, and many of my closest friends have died. It would be rude to ignore them." Sensei's eyes twinkle. "I hope you won't stop talking to me when I die."

Mikko sticks his thumbs into his ears and waggles his fingers. "*Whoooo-ooo,* I'm a ghost," he wails. "I want to talk to Kyoko."

We laugh, and Kyoko kicks Mikko in the shins. But I'm not so sure Sensei was joking. If he really is a *tengu* goblin priest, he would have conversations with the spirits all the time.

As for me, I don't think I could trust anyone I could see straight through. No matter how well mannered they are.

"Phew. What's that smell?" Taji interrupts my thoughts, his nose toward the valley.

Yoshi sniffs. "I can't smell anything."

Neither can I, but that's not surprising. Taji's nose is always first to the finish line. "Smells like . . ."

"Niya's slipper?" suggests Mikko.

Taji pinches his nostrils tight. "It's worse than that."

"Dead fish." I grin, whacking Mikko across the shoulder with an imaginary bundle of them.

"Oh, yuck." Kyoko wrinkles her nose in disgust as the smell grows stronger.

Choking and sputtering, I struggle to breathe. The White Crane isn't brave anymore. Hiding its head under a wing, it refuses to come out.

"*Aaaah.* Sulfur. More pungent than a bottle of medicinal wine," Sensei says, inhaling deeply. "Even the bravest tracker would hesitate to follow us in here."

No one would think we would dare enter this valley.

"Chop, chop, Little Cockroaches. The drum is still beating even though we can no longer hear it. We have only nine days left. No time to hesitate." Sensei takes another step, and the mist reaches out to swallow him whole. "A samurai warrior must not allow himself to be beaten by his nose," he calls.

"A good student doesn't hesitate to follow the teacher. How far will you follow me?" Sensei once asked.

"All the way to hell and back," Yoshi answered for us. "We are very good students."

Now the time has come to prove it.

I can put up with the smell, but I can't forget the ghosts. I don't want to be at the end of the line anymore. Yoshi understands, already moving into place behind me. "Thanks, Yosh," I whisper.

We all feel safer with Sensei and Yoshi. Taji links his arm through mine. The earth is warm on the soles of our sandals, and early morning sun gently thaws the night from our backs. Steamy mist thickens into imaginary faces, but Sensei is right: these ghosts are not bothering us. They look, laugh silently, and dissolve away. They were never really there at all.

We all feel safer with Sensei and Yoshi.

"Would the Dragon Master follow us here?" Nezume's eyes scan the sparse clutches of trees.

It's his greatest fear that one day he will have to return to the Dragon Ryu. The Dragon Master didn't want Nezume until Sensei claimed him as a Cockroach. Now every month the Dragon sends a letter demanding the return of "his boy." Each time Sensei gives the same reply: "Poor handwriting. More practice needed."

"The Dragon Master will not find us here," Sensei promises. "I do not need to see him to know his thoughts. They never change. He will already be on his way to thwart our plans, but as always he travels a different path from me. We'll meet him at the castle."

Sensei smiles as if he's going to meet old friends. But the Emperor and the Dragon Master are powerful foes. Ki-Yaga will need more than a tree frog grin. He'll need two heads, one for each enemy to keep.

We've been walking for half the night and all the morning. Muscles hurt, eyes ache, and the thick air clogs our throats. We are no longer laughing and jostling. Instead, we drag our tired feet through the sticky mud. Grandfather's stories of this place can't be right. Not even dead souls would hang around here.

The trees have shrunk and thinned. Grass has given way to stone. In the beginning, the Tateyama Mountains were born of fire. Now their volcanic heart pulses where patches of mud bubble like thick rice porridge. But no one would come running for a bowl of this foul-smelling sludge, no matter how hungry they were.

"Walking is so boring," Mikko moans.

"A shortcut would be good," adds Nezume.

When we found Nezume on our way to the Annual Trainee Games, he showed us a quicker way into the mountain. Now the Long-Tailed Rat knows all the tracks and trails around the *ryu,* but this valley is a strange, alien place.

The mist wraps across our eyes like a *hachimaki* headband.

"I can't see very well," Yoshi complains.

"Lucky you," laughs Taji. "I can't see at all."

Even Taji's humor can't lift our spirits out of the mud. The White Crane's wings are wet and heavy. The Rat's tail is covered in slime, and the Tiger's fur is matted.

"There's nothing but mud and rocks," Kyoko grumps.

"Then we will walk another way," says Sensei. "It is good to practice."

I groan. There are thirty-three ways to walk, and Sensei makes us learn every one.

"We will walk like a wild cat," he announces. His long legs stretch out in loping strides. We pad after him, but it's not easy to copy.

"Your choice next, Nezume," Sensei instructs.

"Walk like a mouse."

Of course a Rat would say that.

We take small, soundless steps. It's hard with only one leg, but Sensei doesn't let me complain.

"When a one-legged boy creeps, he makes half as much noise," Sensei told me once. "One leg is not an excuse. It is a reason to be proud."

Now it's Mikko's turn to choose.

"Walk like a wild boar," he shouts.

Boars *like* mud. Crashing and blundering, we make more noise than Black Tusk, the wild boar who once stalked the forests around the *ryu*—until Sensei cooked roast pork for dinner. We're making enough noise to wake the dead. I scan the trees, just in case.

My foot aches. My shoulders hurt.

"Are we stopping to rest soon, Sensei?" Yoshi asks.

"I see I am not the only mind reader. Excellent." Our teacher points to a pool of water just ahead. "We are almost there."

We forget our sore muscles and race ahead to look.

"This is a heated mineral pool," Sensei says, easily catching up to us on his thin spider legs. "The water springs from the warm soul of the earth to heal tired joints and cold bones."

"Have we got time for this?" asks Taji, wistfully. He wants to swim, but the drum is pounding inside his head, too.

"After we rest here, we will be able to walk much faster," Sensei promises.

That's all the encouragement we need.

Nezume kicks off his sandals and dips a toe into the pool. A grin ripples across his face.

Kyoko cups a handful of the water, and her Snow Monkey spirit smiles mischievously. "You try it." She flicks the water into my face and up my nose. "That's for pulling my hair yesterday. Now we're even."

I should have known I couldn't outsmart her.

"The ninja come here often," says Sensei. "Unlike

my samurai kids, they love to bathe. A clean person has no odor and cannot be identified when disguised. We can learn much from the study of the ninja arts."

Sensei said the ninja are not our enemies. I trust him, but the ninja are not my friends, either. I'm not ready to learn anything from them yet. How can it be right to sneak and deceive? When I draw my sword in battle, the White Crane will screech and I'll shout my name proudly for all to hear. Grandfather says the ninja are part demon and part man, part magic and part trickery. They would fit right in in Hell Valley.

"Are there ninja here now?" Yoshi's eyes comb the straggly-haired trees. "I'd like to meet one."

My eyes follow his. "I don't see anyone."

And I don't want to meet one.

"There's nowhere for a ninja to hide here," says Nezume.

Sensei points to the nearest rock. "A ninja doesn't need to hide to conceal himself. Does a moth hide away when camouflaged against the tree trunk? The ninja way is one of *budo,* of blending into his surroundings. Are you sure that's really a rock?"

"I'll check," Mikko volunteers with a grin. He gives it a kick.

"*Ow-aw*. It's a rock!" he yelps, hopping around as if he were me.

"What about that one?" Sensei points again.

But Mikko cannot kick rocks all the way to the castle.

"I think there were five ninja following us." Taji listens and sniffs. "But they are not here now."

"I'm sure they have better things to do than watch my students wash." Hanging his sword and staff on a tree branch, Sensei throws his kimono, jacket, and trousers onto a large flat rock.

Sensei is chopstick-thin, like rice paper stretched over chicken bone. This time I'm not fooled by what I can see. The Dragon Master is younger and strong as an oak tree. But when he challenged Sensei at the Games, our teacher whirled his bamboo staff and that oak tree crashed into the dirt.

The first pool flows into an even deeper one, wide enough to swim and play in. Sensei steps into the shallows, then wades out until only his head is showing.

Carefully, we place our swords in the tree, too. Then we toss our clothes on top of Sensei's jacket. Shivering in my long undershirt and loincloth, I throw my crutch down as well. But I miss the clothes, and it bounces off the rock to land in the stringy branches of a small tree. It's the perfect place for anyone or anything to hide. I have to go get it, but I stall by pulling on my robe and grabbing my sword.

"Do you want me to come with you?" Mikko calls from the water. Mikko and I tease each other all the time, but we know when to stop. That's how the lines of friendship are drawn: in exactly the right place.

"I'm okay," I call, already halfway to the tree. Taji said the ninja had gone, and so far I haven't seen a single ghost.

Except for the one sitting on the bottom branch, holding my crutch.

CHAPTER FIVE

義

WHAT THE
GHOST SAID

Red-hot eyes burn through me. The White Crane cringes and pulls its wings in close, away from the heat. My stomach cramps tighter than a tangled kite string.

"Nice weather, isn't it?" The ghost's words whistle through missing teeth.

I shiver. "Very n-nice."

"You should be more careful." It passes me my crutch. "Dead people don't like to be hit in the head with lumps of wood. Didn't you see me sitting here?"

"S-s-sorry. Thank you."

The ghost nods, accepting my apology. "Some people don't even believe I exist. Like your friends. They can't see me because they won't look. I don't like being ignored." Angry now, its voice hisses like steam. "Nobody wants to fade away to nothing. Not even a ghost."

Sensei told us that a samurai warrior must stand straight and still when he looks into the face of death. Now I understand why. It's easier to stand still when you're scared stiff.

"Would you like it if people looked straight through you?" the ghost demands.

I shake my head politely, trying not to stare. But my eyelids are frozen open in fright. Grandfather told me that ghosts like gruesome meals. In Grandfather's stories, their caves are littered with the bones of kids just like me. My teeth chatter.

"Are you cold?" Its voice curdles, sour as overheated milk. "If you take my hand, you'll feel warm."

I can see only two fingers and a shard of broken bone. The hand is a lump of melted flesh.

I'm not touching that.

Fiery eyes spit and crackle, but I'm shivering so hard that my head shakes without me. "N-no. I'm fine. Thank you."

The ghost nods approvingly in Sensei's direction. "Ki-Yaga always teaches his students good manners."

Looking up, Sensei waves. I should have known he could see what was happening. The wizard sees everything, even with eyes closed, asleep under the old cherry tree back at the *ryu*.

Fear is nothing to be afraid of, Sensei whispers inside my head. *And except for a little leftover skin and bone, a ghost is all hot air.*

Braver now, the White Crane unfolds one wing. I place my hand on my sword. Onaku's blade cannot cut through what is hardly there, but with my fingers around the hilt and Sensei's words in my head, I feel less afraid.

I'm not out of the trees and into the pool yet. The ghost grins, its mouth a grotesque cave of bones. "I have a message for you."

I don't want to know.

It leans closer, hot breath in my ear. My heart beats like the mountain drum. *Thum. Ta-thum. Thum-thum-thump.* I'm afraid to listen, but there's no escape.

"You need only one slipper." The ghost's voice cackles softly, embers in a dying fire.

"What?" The ghost is making fun of me! My blood bubbles in anger. I'm not afraid anymore. No one likes to be made a fool of. Especially me. The other *ryu*s always jeer and call me silly names. Hopscotch. Frog foot. I'm glad I whacked the ghost in the head with my crutch. I'd like to do it again.

But now the branch is empty. All that remains is the faint smell of scorched wood.

"Come back," I yell, swinging my crutch like a sword. "Who are you to laugh at my one leg when your body is barely there? You're nothing but a pair of firefly eyes."

A Cockroach is not afraid of other bugs.

"What was all that yelling about?" Nezume asks moments later when I climb into the pool, my crutch safely leaning against our clothes.

Kyoko giggles. "Niya likes to talk to himself."

"So who was he waving his crutch at?" asks Mikko, snickering.

I'd do more than wave my crutch at him, if it wasn't resting out of reach. "Didn't you see anything?" I ask.

My friends shake their heads.

"Niya was talking to ghosts." Mikko laughs at his joke, and Nezume joins in, even louder.

Sensei says nothing, but his face has words written all over it. My friends can read the whole story there. It's not a joke. Their eyes grow as wide and round as rice balls.

"Were you scared?" Kyoko's eyes are biggest of all.

"No. I stood straight and still like a samurai warrior. I stared death in the face." Even Mikko looks impressed. "I shook my crutch, and it ran away."

It's almost true. Most of the time I was so terrified I couldn't move. But in the end, I did shake my crutch. They all saw that.

"What did the ghost say?" Yoshi asks.

Embarrassed, I stare down at my foot. "It said, 'You need only one slipper.'"

"I could have told you that without even looking," Taji says with a hoot.

Kyoko tries to hide her giggle behind her hand, but Yoshi guffaws loudly. Nezume and Mikko slap palms. Even Sensei thinks it's funny.

When the ghost laughed at me, I was insulted. But when my friends laugh, it sounds different. It makes me smile and forget my anger.

"The dead like to play games, but they are also very knowledgeable. The ghost has given Niya a special message," Sensei says. "Sometimes the information we need is right under our foot."

"But what does the message mean, Sensei?" asks Yoshi.

"It means Niya has a task to complete. And he only needs one slipper to do it."

"Maybe Niya will stop the war with his smelly old slipper," Mikko teases.

I wish it was that easy. I would give my remaining foot to ensure no one dies.

Inside my head, the wizard is whispering again: *I am very proud. You have passed an important test. None of my other students were ready.*

The pool soothes my aching muscles, but Sensei's words warm my heart. I want to ask more questions. Why am I being tested? What task must I complete? And why do I need to be told what I can see every morning when I put my slipper on? But there's an even more important question I need to ask Sensei. "Are you worried about what will happen when we reach the castle, Master?"

I know *I* am. What would we do without Sensei? Yoshi is a good leader, but he's not a teacher. And we still have so much to learn.

"There is nothing to fear. The Emperor is wise but very superstitious, and he knows that if he chopped off my head, I would haunt him for the rest of his life." Sensei smiles. "He would never enter Hell Valley. One word from a ghost and the Son of Heaven would die of fright."

"I could stay here forever," Kyoko sighs. Her long white hair floats like water lilies on the surface of the pool.

Taji sinks low until only frog eyes show above the water. "The ninja are smart to come here."

Not even I would argue with that. The waters of the river near the *ryu* are freezing cold, except in the middle of summer. But the mineral pool is the color of tea and just as warming.

Nezume pulls my foot out from under me, and I sink toward the bottom. When I surface, thrashing and sputtering, I spit water in Nezume's face. Despite appearances, mineral water is not good to drink—it doesn't *taste* a thing like tea.

"I like the feel of warm mud between my toes," says Nezume. "Maybe I would like to be a ninja."

I shake my head. "The ninja sneaks around in the night, but the samurai calls his challenge loud and brave, looking his opponent in the eye."

Sensei smiles knowingly, like the cat that swallowed the crane. "If you are hungry for an extra rice cake and there is only one left over, what do you do? Do you wave your sword and shout for challengers?"

I remember the honey rice cakes we had for dessert two nights ago. Especially the last one I ate in secret as I sat on the *ryu* kitchen floor in the moonlight. Sensei knows what I did. I sneaked in, just like a ninja.

"Sometimes ninja skills might be useful," I admit.

Taji pokes me in the ribs. "Next you'll be throwing *shuriken* stars."

Shuriken stars are small metal shapes the ninja use to throw or stab. They can be tossed at the eyes, hands, or feet, and they're used to distract a warrior from his sword. I lean back against the edge of the pool, warm water lapping against my chin.

Someone pulls my hair. Hard.

I ignore it. Then it happens again, even harder.

I whirl around to face Kyoko. "You said we were even. Why are you pulling my hair?"

"I didn't do anything." She grins. "Although I wish I did. Maybe it was ninja fingers."

"Or a ghost. *Whooooo . . .*" Yoshi teases.

Another tug. This time I'm faster and find myself looking at a bunch of tiny faces with more wrinkles than Sensei and breath worse than one of Uma's after-dinner belches.

"Snow monkeys!" Kyoko shouts excitedly.

She was born in the snow-covered mountains of northernmost Honshu. Her superstitious parents left their white-haired, six-fingered child on the mountainside to die. The snow monkeys came and

"Snow monkeys!" Kyoko shouts excitedly.

took her to their home—and that's where Sensei found her, climbing trees before she was old enough to walk.

"Look, Sensei, there are five. It's a family." Kyoko reaches out to link fingers with the mother.

"Five is a good number. My favorite," Sensei says, gently removing a young monkey from the top of his head.

Two bigger monkeys fight over who will pull my hair next. They chatter and screech. They chase their tails around the pool and stick their noses in our clothes.

Nezume laughs. "They're checking to see who smells the worst."

"That'll be Niya. You don't have to be a ninja to smell him coming," Mikko teases.

I've only got one foot, but it kicks twice as hard. Even underwater.

"Er-er-ergh," Mikko groans theatrically and does a dead-fish impersonation, floating on top of the water.

"I do not smell. And no one can tell who a person is by sniffing," I insist. "Not even a ninja. Or Taji. Or a monkey."

The smallest snow monkey pushes its way into my armpit to prove me wrong.

"Every person has their own odor." Taji smiles. "You know that." He blows a kiss to remind me. Mrs. Onaku smells like cherry blossoms.

"The ninja have many secrets worth learning," Sensei says. "Before I came to the Cockroach Ryu, I trained with a ninjutsu master for more than a decade."

Sensei is a samurai and a ninja? Wait till Grandfather hears about this. It'll make a great story.

"I learned to move with the wind, to disappear in the mist, and to run up the cherry tree. How do you think I manage such things? Did you think I could do magic?"

I *know* he can. I know because he's always practicing on me. Maybe I could learn a little ninja magic too. Then when Kyoko throws things at us, she won't be able to escape by climbing Sensei's cherry tree. I'll be able to run up after her.

"You would make a good ninja, Taji." Sensei's praise fills Taji's unseeing eyes with pride.

"What about me?" I ask. Before, I mocked the ninja. I only wanted to yell and wave my sword. But now, suddenly, I want to do more. I want to sneak and sniff and fade into the night. Like Sensei.

"You are an excellent student, Niya. Even ghosts want to teach you a lesson. You could learn to be the greatest ninjutsu samurai ever."

Even better than Sensei? *Not likely.* But in my heart I accept the challenge and the wizard nods.

"Are there any ninja girls?" Kyoko asks.

Sensei smiles. "Many more than samurai girls."

Kyoko is the only samurai girl we've ever heard of.

"There are?" Mikko grins and whistles. "Then I think I might be a ninja, too."

Sensei closes his eyes and twists the water from his long white beard. We wait for his words of wisdom to fall with a splash. Even the snow monkeys are quiet now.

"We must learn to open our eyes and ears to new things if we are to stop the war drum. Our first battle is not far away."

Yoshi looks alarmed. "I thought we weren't fighting."

"Not every conflict is settled with a sword. At the castle, a word can send a head rolling across the floor," Sensei says.

The White Crane cowers. Is Sensei talking about his own head? He smiles at me, but I don't feel reassured.

"Our path to Toyozawa is very rocky," Sensei continues.

"I know." Mikko grimaces. His foot still hurts from kicking rocks.

Sensei stretches his arm out, palm down. *"Chi,"* he says.

Yoshi places his hand over Sensei's and Taji adds his next. *"Jin."*

Then Kyoko. Mikko. And me. *"Yu."*

Chi, jin, yu.

Wisdom, benevolence, and courage.

Our wet hands form a mountain where the code of the samurai binds us together. Ancient powerful words, stronger than rock and sharper than any sword. Standing together, samurai kids are not afraid of anything. I'm even braver than the Emperor of Japan. Not even the most fearsome ghost in Hell Valley could frighten me now.

CHAPTER SIX

礼

THE BACK ROAD
TO TOYOZAWA

"Drop," Sensei yells.

We do, without hesitation or thought for rocks, mud, and puddles. We sit cross-legged and still and wait for the next instruction. We've been doing this training exercise since our first day together at the *ryu*. A samurai cannot choose where to fight his battles, so Sensei doesn't let us pick where we practice. Anywhere will do. Even in the middle of the back road to Toyozawa.

I watch Sensei's eyes, searching for the moment when he will command us to jump up and draw our swords. Flickering eyes mean your opponent is thinking. When a man makes a decision, his eyes stop moving. He doesn't need to think anymore. He knows.

"The samurai who draws first is very slow," Sensei taught us. "He draws first because he needs a head start. The true swordsman waits until the last moment, then unsheathes so fast that he catches his opponent in mid-swing."

My leg aches, but I don't move. Beside me Nezume crouches motionless, coiled to spring at Sensei's next word. Like his spirit totem, the Long-Tailed Rat, Nezume radiates nervous energy. Nose twitching, ears wriggling. He'd flick his tail, too, if he had one.

Nezume has the fastest sword in the mountains; he always draws last and slices first. No wonder the Dragon Master wants him back. He doesn't want Nezume on our team at the Games next year.

"Draw!" Sensei bellows.

I'm on my foot in an instant, sword in hand. Yoshi is standing too close, and I catch him on the elbow by accident. It's a good thing we are using our wooden swords for practice, or Yoshi would have nothing to lean on next time he lies out on his rock overlooking the valley. But it's my error. To bump against another samurai is a great insult. Honor demands a duel to the death. Luckily, to bump against a samurai kid is not as dangerous.

Yoshi pokes his tongue out at me, raising his sword in triumph. "Niya loses a point."

We don't really keep score. Sensei doesn't believe in awarding prizes. When we asked for merit scrolls like the other *ryu*s have, he gave each of us a blank piece of rice paper.

"This contains everything I have taught you," he said, presenting my copy with a flourish and a smile.

I grinned back. "Then I am an excellent student, because I have learned it all."

Awards look good, but they mean nothing. Still, we did like winning the trophy at the Annual Samurai Trainee Games. And there is one reward worth striving for. When Sensei beams at us with pleasure, we glow warm and proud.

"Stop," Sensei commands.

We turn to stone, like statues blocking the road. Sensei usually waits until one of us moves. Usually Kyoko will giggle or Nezume will twitch his nose, but sometimes it takes hours. This afternoon, Sensei doesn't have the whole day to wait. *Ta-thum. Thum. Thump.* Inside my head, the drum throbs against my temples. Time is running out. Only eight days left.

"Go!" Sensei yells.

We take off running. The road winds through the rice fields where the only people we'll see will be farmers, too busy to notice an old man and his students. It takes a lot of rice to feed a castle town and to pay its samurai soldiers. Once the samurai lived on country estates, but peace has made the daimyos nervous and they like to keep their armies close. Now most of the samurai live in houses in the town or castle keep, their wages paid in rice. Their jobs are to wait and practice.

No wonder Sensei makes us train so hard. We are practicing for a life of practice.

"More practice," Sensei yells. "Run like the tiger."

Yoshi *is* the Tiger, and with great loping strides, he hunts down Sensei. The rest of us chase along behind. We're covering ground quickly now. At this pace, we might even reach the castle town by midnight.

My father is a town samurai. He collects his samurai rice and lives in a comfortable house with a garden. But sometimes I know he wishes for the days of Grandfather's youth, when samurai slept in fields. One winter, Grandfather told us he slept in the snow. "*Brrr!* Too cold for me. I'm glad we don't do that anymore," Father said. But he doesn't want to grow old counting rice, either.

Sensei slows to a brisk walk. "Soon we will reach the river," he says. "We'll stop and catch fish for dinner."

None of us are fooled by that. He means he'll sleep on the riverbank while we hold the rods. Fishing is so boring. Mikko groans and Nezume moans even louder.

"I can't see the point of fishing," Taji complains.

Kyoko giggles. It's a good joke because Taji can't see anything.

"It is a waste of time," I agree. "I thought we were in a hurry."

"The war will not outrun the drumbeat, and we do not want to stand before the Emperor without the skills we need. All samurai warriors have time to fish," Sensei insists. "It's always good practice."

Not more practice.

Even Yoshi rolls his eyes, but Sensei continues. "It keeps the brain focused. If a samurai allows his brain to wander off, when it comes back, there will be no head left to hold it. Fishing teaches the mind to stay in one place."

I'm not convinced. Fishing puts my brain to sleep. And I'll bet it does the same for Sensei. That's probably why he lies there snoring while we cast our lines.

Sensei's smile flashes in my eyes like sunlight on fish scales. He knows what I'm thinking.

When we reach the place where the road crosses the river, Sensei stops to talk to a lone man fishing on the bridge. He bows low and exchanges a bottle of wine for a bucket of bait. The only way to catch a river sweetfish is with another of its kind. Sweetfish are too smart to swallow a hook but foolish enough to chase the bait fish.

The road soon veers from the flat, open fields to the protection of trees.

"Stop!" Sensei yells.

Yoshi crashes into me. I stumble against Mikko, who tips over. He falls, dragging Taji and me with him. Kyoko loses her footing, and Nezume lands on top of us all.

Only Sensei is still standing.

"We thought you said 'drop,'" Mikko says sheepishly.

"I can't hear anything. Someone's elbow is in my ear," Taji complains.

"Sorry," Yoshi and Kyoko chorus.

Poor Taji. One elbow in each ear.

"We have found the perfect spot," Sensei announces over the noise of arms and legs untangling.

Nezume removes his foot from my face, just in time. I was about to bite it.

"Are there lots of fish here?" he asks.

"Even more important. There is a tree," Sensei says, settling back against it. "Fish swim all over the river, so it does not matter where you throw your line. A tree is much harder to catch. You must find a place where one is already standing still."

That's true, but I'd rather chase trees than fish any day.

Sensei unties the long bundle from his back and takes out our rods. My mouth waters. Fresh sweetfish taste much better than two-day-old rice cakes, cold omelette, and gluey noodles. Sensei will let us light a cooking fire this evening. Last night, on the edge of Hell Valley, we slept on warm volcanic rocks around the hot springs, but our food was stone cold. Sensei said flames might attract attention. Here on the road, many fires burn through the night. One more won't be noticed.

Inside the bucket are six small sweetfish, one for each of our hooks. The first fish is the bait to catch the second. Then the second fish becomes the bait to catch the third. That's if any of us get up to three. Sweetfish are not easy to catch.

I cast my rod into the river wearily. I'm tired of this already.

"Look, Niya." Mikko points to a bird upriver at the far water's edge. It's a white crane.

We creep closer. Head bent slightly, the crane stands

perfectly still, black eyes staring into the water. Even the crane must concentrate when fishing. At the last moment it strikes, faster than a samurai sword stroke. When it lifts its beak out of the water, a bright silver fish struggles in its mouth.

"Why can't you do that?" Yoshi teases me. "Then we wouldn't have to stand around fishing so long."

I would if I could. Anything to spend less time fishing.

My friends drift back toward Sensei and their rods. But the white crane holds me in place. It turns and looks. Standing straight and still, I raise my arms high.

"Aye-ee-yah." I am the White Crane.

Aye-ee-yah. The other crane screeches in response, opening its wings wide and lifting itself into the sky. I watch it wheel over the river and head toward the town, the castle, and the ocean. My thoughts soar after it: *I'll see you there. I can't fly yet, but I'm coming, too.*

"It's very beautiful." Kyoko's voice makes me jump. Not easy on one foot.

"So graceful," she sighs. "Can I tell you a secret? You mustn't tell anyone. Not even Sensei."

"Okay." It's easy to agree. Whatever it is, Sensei already knows. He always does.

Kyoko smiles. Hesitates. Then blurts, "Sometimes I wish I was beautiful."

I don't know what to say, because she already is. I try to remember the words from one of the haiku poems we studied. That would help. But I always fall asleep in poetry class. It's even more tedious than fishing. But right now I wish I'd paid more attention.

Kyoko shifts uncomfortably in the silence. "Forget what I told you," she says, reaching out to grab the front of my jacket and twist it tightly. "All right?"

"Okay," I agree again. It's hard not to, with her fist in front of my nose.

"What did I say?" she demands.

"When?"

It's the right answer, and Kyoko lets go of my jacket. "Thanks, Niya." She turns and runs to join the others. A samurai girl is much harder to understand than any haiku.

"Got one," Yoshi booms.

Not even Sensei could sleep through that, but his wizard eyes stay closed. They'll open like magic the moment we have just enough fish. They always do.

"I've got one, too," Nezume shouts.

It's still another hour before we've caught enough. Kyoko strings the last one onto a long stick. Sensei's eyes snap open.

"More walking, more practice," he says, jumping to his feet and rapping his staff on the ground.

The last few days we have traveled the back road, skulked through the late afternoon or walked in the darkness. It's dusk now. The road is almost empty because closer to town, it's no longer safe. This is the hour when merchants and travelers hurry to their lodgings before the gangs of outlaws and robbers slink from the shadows. But samurai kids aren't scared of anything except haiku lessons.

Here the road is paved. It's easier for me to walk on the cobblestones, and the clip of my crutch has a familiar ring. I was born in a town, but none of my friends have even seen a road before. Their homes are in small villages with dirt paths and mountain tracks.

Taji tips his head sideways, the way he does when he's listening hard for something. Have the ninjas and spies finally caught up with us? Sensei isn't worried. He strides, whistling, his long legs hurrying us along. I decide not to worry, either. I'll find out soon enough.

"Halt!"

Ten men block our way, roadside cutthroats whose swords glimmer, dull and greedy.

Sensei says nothing, eyes measuring the man in front of him.

"Give us those sweetfish and everything else you have," the leader says, "or I will slice you and the kids where you stand."

We move as one to protect our teacher and defend our honor. But Sensei waves us back, his gesture telling us to sit on the grass and wait.

"Do you have any more men to help you?" our master asks politely.

The man sees an old fool when he looks at Sensei. It's his first mistake.

"Why?" he growls, amused.

"Because I have you outnumbered. It would not be a fair fight when you have only ten men to fight against me."

Ki-Yaga is a master swordsman who could cut down this band of vagabonds blindfolded, with one arm tied

Ki-Yaga is a master swordsman who could cut
down this band of vagabonds blindfolded.

behind his back and one leg tucked up. He draws his blade so fast, it is only a flash of light until it rests, point hard against the big man's stomach.

This bunch is not stupid after all. The big man sees what he is up against. He bows low and edges back into the forest, taking his followers with him.

Sensei tucks his blade into his sash and waves us forward. We hurry to keep up.

In a small cleared area nearby, Sensei stops.

"Shouldn't we keep walking?" I ask. I see danger everywhere now.

"Time for dinner," he says. "Not even I can stop a war on an empty stomach."

Or without a head. Suddenly, I'm not in such a hurry to reach the castle. We quickly gather branches and sticks. Our teacher eyes them with a smile.

"No, not now," I groan. Sometimes I can read Sensei's mind, too. He thinks we should do *bo* practice. Fighting with sticks. It's all about dodging, ducking, weaving. And one well-timed blow.

"A samurai may not always have his sword," Sensei teaches us. "But he can always find a stick."

We don't argue. Once Mikko did. "A samurai can't

always find a stick. There are no sticks here in the classroom," he had said.

Sensei then picked up the broom and Mikko ducked. *Bo* training had begun.

While we practice, Sensei cooks. After dinner we lie back under the stars and dread the night's walk ahead.

"I am so tired, I think I will sleepwalk to the castle." Yoshi yawns.

"It's safe here," Sensei says. "We can stay tonight."

We're almost used to sleeping in the day, but rest seems more comfortable and familiar under a blanket of darkness.

"Dream deep, Little Cockroaches. I am going for a walk." Taking his staff, Sensei heads in the direction of the river.

Our master often walks alone at night. The others know what I think of that.

"Sensei's gone for his evening fly around the mountains." Mikko jabs me in the ribs.

"It might be true," I say. "I'm not the only one who thinks so. Down in the village the old women say Sensei is a *tengu*."

"Old wives' tales. Now Niya is an old woman." Yoshi laughs.

My friends are probably right. A *tengu* is a mountain goblin priest, a samurai who has fallen from grace. But Sensei is good, kind, and wiser than the mountains.

"What could Sensei have done?" Kyoko asks. "It would have to have been something truly dreadful."

"The most dreadful," agrees Nezume.

We know what that would have to be. Every samurai kid does. It's the first thing a father teaches his child. "The most dishonorable thing a samurai can do is to share the sky with the man who killed his father."

"It can't be that," Yoshi says. "Sensei would not hesitate to avenge his father's honor."

And he would never shirk his duty. Even though he teaches us that our swords should not be used for killing unless absolutely necessary, we know that Sensei has killed many men in battle.

"Go to sleep," Taji grumbles. "Why are we even discussing this? Sometimes I think you have bean sprouts for brains, Niya."

Yoshi chuckles. I've always been the quickest thinker, and my friends are proud of that. But it doesn't stop them from giggling at me. Laughter between friends is a double-edged sword, held carefully so it does no harm.

The night quickly fills with snuffles and snores. Except mine. Sleeps runs ahead of me, and no matter how fast I hop, I can't catch up to it. Under the full moon the White Crane is restless. I pull my blanket over my head, but it doesn't help.

Hours later Sensei slips noiselessly back to settle against his cherry tree. In the moonlight I see his closed lids.

"Are you having trouble sleeping?" he asks me.

"Yes, Sensei," I admit.

"Then you must ask the question that is keeping you awake. Only then will you be able to sleep."

It's not easy to ask. "Can you fly, Sensei?"

"Everyone who dreams can fly," he answers.

The White Crane nods drowsily.

"Can you sleep now, Niya?"

"Yes, Master."

I close my eyes and dream I can fly.

CHAPTER SEVEN

勇

GRANDFATHER'S
STORIES

Last night I dreamed I soared above the fields, over the town, and across the ocean. But when I woke this morning, the castle was still a day's walk away. Sensei sets a fast pace, and we hurry along behind, telling stories about all the things we'll see and do when we reach the Emperor's court. No one mentions the terrible things that might happen.

Instead of taking the quickest route, Sensei veers right, onto a lesser road. Here the cobblestones are overgrown with grass and the road is empty. Safe.

"This is the way to my home," I announce excitedly.

"Why are we going there?" asks Taji.

I shrug. "I don't know. Maybe Father invited us."

"Ask Sensei," Kyoko suggests. My friends are listening closely, but Sensei strides ahead, out of earshot.

He doesn't need ears to listen. "I must ask Niya's Grandfather for news of the castle. It is an advantage to know before we arrive."

Ha! Sensei doesn't know everything after all.

But the wizard does know what I'm thinking and his blue eyes drill into mine.

"A samurai must be prepared. Swordsmanship is not

everything. In battle it is sometimes useful to know on what day your opponent was born."

We wait for Sensei's lesson to solve our puzzled faces.

"Even the fiercest warrior will hesitate and smile if you yell 'happy birthday,'" Sensei says, swinging an imaginary sword to make us duck. "He who hesitates has lost. And often what he has lost is his head."

It's hard to believe that Grandfather knows any useful information. He is not wise like Sensei. He stands straight and his eyes are clear, but his mind is bent and muddled. Wisdom came with age, but it left with even older age. Sometimes, for no reason, Grandfather laughs in the middle of a sentence. And sometimes he disappears for days.

"Where has Grandfather gone?" I would ask my father.

He'd smile and say, "Our Eldest One is like the wind. He blows out and he blows in."

Father never seemed worried, and he was right. The wind always returned. And so did Grandfather.

"My grandfather will not be much help," I confess. "He tells many stories, but they're not all true."

Sensei grins. "Like the tale of the imaginary ghosts

of Hell Valley? The best place to hide a fact is behind a screen of fiction."

Grandfather *was* right about the ghosts. I think back over all the other stories he told me. Shape-shifters. Wizards. *Tengu* goblins of the mountain. Maybe *he* can tell me a story about Sensei.

"I can't wait to meet your sister. I'm bored with boy talk." Kyoko covers her ears, pretending to be in pain.

"You'll be disappointed," I yell. "Ayame talks endlessly about dolls and spends all day changing their kimonos and braiding their hair."

I laugh at the faces Kyoko makes. My sister, Ayame, is soft and fragile like a flower. She's not like Kyoko at all. Ayame couldn't kick her way out of a rice-paper bag.

"As long as the pillows are fluffy and my bed is warm, I don't care how many giggling girls I have to put up with," Mikko says. "I'm tired of sleeping on the ground."

"I can't wait to see the town. What's it like?" asks Yoshi.

"People rush everywhere. They are busy like bees, packed tighter than honeycomb in the hive," Sensei says.

The others gather around, hanging on every word.

"When I went to bed, I could hear the people next door snoring," I tell them.

Nezume laughs. "I bet they could hear you snoring ten houses away."

"I don't snore," I insist.

But when Sensei nods, I decide not to protest so loudly.

"I thought we didn't want people to know where we were," says Taji. "Why are we going into such a crowded place?"

It's a good question. Walls have ears, and a town is nothing but rows and rows of listening walls.

"If you don't want to be found, where is the best place to hide?" Sensei asks.

Taji knows that, of course. "Where no one would look."

Pleased, our teacher claps his hands. "Excellent. No one would ever expect us to go to Niya's home."

It's true. Not even I did.

"The ninja will," Yoshi teases. "I bet they're watching now."

Mikko brandishes his sword at the nearest rock. "Come out and show yourself."

"The ninja creep like the wind. No one can hide from that," Sensei agrees. "But we have nothing to fear from them either."

My thoughts are warmed by the fire waiting for us at home. Around me my friends chatter about market stalls and how many types of sweets the vendors might sell. Their cheeks are full of imaginary balls of cherry blossom gum.

But one question bothers me. "Do Mother and Father know we are coming, Sensei?"

My parents are very proud that the great Ki-Yaga chose to teach me. But Mother has a voice like a bird and she never stops singing. If she knows we're coming, it will be all over the tearooms, from one end of Japan to the other. Everyone will know where we are.

Sensei smiles into my eyes, and his voice is a shadow against my ear. "Your grandfather will tell them when we are closer."

How can he? He doesn't know.

I will tell him, the wizard whispers inside my head. *Just like this.*

It's almost midnight when we reach the edge of the castle town. I guide my friends through the dark, narrow streets toward my home. We trudge past rows of houses, stacked and packed like origami boxes.

The way of the warrior is a long walk. So many paths to travel — Buddha, Tao, Zen. We walk in never-ending circles until our brains spin like goldfish swimming in a bowl.

"When you have lost your place in the world, you are enlightened and your mind will triumph in battle," Sensei taught us.

That's good news for me. I've got a terrible sense of direction, and I get lost often. I'm on the fast track to enlightenment and victory.

But tonight our walking is almost over.

"Are you nervous?" whispers Kyoko.

"Just a little." I haven't seen my family for years.

Yoshi puts his arm around my shoulders for support. Friends make the best crutches.

Memories rewind inside my head. Father painting. Mother's song as she sweeps. Ayame playing with her dolls and Grandfather dozing in the garden.

"Here we are." I knock gently, and Mother opens the door. Her arms wrap me up like a present.

"Welcome, Ki-Yaga." Father bows. "My home is yours tonight. I am proud to have so many sons and daughters." He nods in my direction, a small nod, hardly noticeable. But I understand what it means. He's especially proud of me. The White Crane preens, fluffing its feathers.

"Your house is huge," Kyoko whispers.

It never seemed that way to me. Our house being on the outskirts of town means that Father is not an important samurai. Not influential or wealthy enough to live inside the castle walls. But the buildings of the *ryu* have only one room and my house has seven. More rooms than Kyoko has ever seen.

Father ushers us into the main room, where Grandfather and Ayame are waiting. My little sister wears a pink kimono and shimmers like a spray of cherry blossoms.

Sensei and Grandfather bow low, scraping their foreheads on Mother's perfectly swept floors.

When I used to laugh at her constant dusting and cleaning, she scolded me.

"We must do things many times to get them right," she said.

And now I understand. Over and over. Round and round. Many paths lead to enlightenment, and my mother sweeps hers clean.

"Our home is bright and shiny," I whisper in Mother's ear. "I am happy to be here."

When Mother smiles at my compliment, the house is even brighter than before.

Grandfather claps his hands. "Now we are together, we must share tea. Ayame will serve us."

"Yes, Eldest One." She bends gracefully.

Kyoko raises an eyebrow in my direction as Ayame leaves to begin the preparations. This is not the irritating little sister I left behind. Tea making is an ancient and sacred ceremony. It requires special skill. Sensei doesn't let any of us touch his tea utensils.

"You are not yet ready," he had said. And he was right. We didn't want to waste our time pouring hot water on dry leaves. But if Ayame can do it, then maybe I can, too.

Sensei nods at me and smiles approvingly into my thoughts.

The entrance to the tearoom is so small that we have to kneel to pass through. Respectfully, Sensei stops in front of the scroll alcove to read the words especially placed there:

The rat scuttles, the big cat creeps, the monkey dashes,
The bat glides, the white crane soars, the lizard darts,
And the owl hoots
In the middle of the night.

We recognize ourselves, but who is the owl?

"Sensei must be the owl," Yoshi whispers. "He's wise."

Nezume agrees. "And he sleeps all day."

"And flies at night, if you ask Niya," adds Mikko.

"*Shh,*" Mother reminds us.

Pausing, Sensei admires the kettle and the hearth. The tea ceremony is a ritual of rules. Even getting to the mat is hard. You have to shuffle slowly. It's bad manners to tread on any lines between the tatami matting squares. When we were little, we used to yell, "The ghosts will get you if you do." But it wasn't ghosts we had to worry about. If you stepped on a line, Father would bellow. Just as scary.

First, Grandfather is seated. Then Sensei, the guest of honor. Father and Mother sit on either side of Sensei. We let Yoshi go next, because he's our leader. Feet tucked under, we rest back on our heels. Samurai kids have been doing this since the day they were born. It's easy, even with one leg.

Grandfather gestures for Ayame to begin. In the moonlight, her eyes glow bright and serious. Placing the tray on the ground, she slowly removes the cloth cover to reveal the tea bowl and tools of my ancestors.

Reverently, Ayame wipes the bowl. Three scoops of tea for each of us. She blends the paste and adds the remaining water. Her hands swirl like magic. Around and around the path.

Grandfather sips, wipes the rim, and hands the bowl to Sensei. Sensei sips, wipes, and passes it to Father. Another circle. Around again. We all take turns. Finally, Grandfather passes the empty bowl to Sensei to admire one last time. Cracked in many places, it has been carefully glued with lacquer and painted over with gold. It's an expensive way to repair an old pot. But I wouldn't dare tell Father that.

When Sensei makes tea, we are allowed to ask questions.

I remember the time I asked, "Why is the tea ceremony so slow?"

"To allow us enough time to treasure each moment," answered Sensei.

I didn't understand and wished it was over. I pinched Mikko sneakily. He pinched me back so hard I spilled my lukewarm tea all over Yoshi. Then Kyoko giggled. Nezume and Taji chuckled.

But Sensei rolled his eyes and said, "We will practice washing up."

Now with all the people I love around me, I finally understand. The room is filled with treasure, and I want this moment to last all night.

But it can't. The drum doesn't stop for cups of tea. There are only seven days left before the war begins. *Ta-thum. Thum. Thump.* Ayame folds her hands, and the ceremony is complete.

We leave the room with our hearts warm and full. Our bellies are still empty, but Mother has supper ready. Steaming noodles in fish broth. Nezume's nose twitches, and Yoshi's stomach growls.

"Your daughter shows much skill," Sensei tells Father and Mother.

My little sister glows pink and proud beneath his praise. My friends and I know exactly how she feels. Sensei's approval is even better than seconds for dessert.

"You should study tea making with a master," I say, impressed.

Ayame shakes her head. "This is enough learning for me. I only wish to pour tea for my husband and his honored guests. I am not going to be a scholar. I'm going to be a rich man's wife."

Someone to keep her in pearls and pink kimonos. She's still a little girl after all. I bet she's got dolls tucked in her sleeves.

"What sort of man would that be?" Sensei smiles. "A samurai swordsman perhaps?"

"A court administrator," says Ayame. "They have big houses filled with gold."

Mikko sputters. "What's wrong with a real samurai? Why would you want to marry a warrior who wields a writing brush?"

Ayame giggles.

I hate writing, but I love listening to stories. Sensei settles back cross-legged, ready to tell one. "When Grandfather was younger, he came on a pilgrimage to the Cockroach Ryu."

Grandfather never told me this story.

"I asked him a *koan*. Like I ask all my students. 'What was your face before you were born?' I said. Your grandfather would make the strangest faces, but he never found the answer." Sensei grins. "Would you like to tell him, Niya?"

"The boy always was twice as clever as me," Grandfather says proudly.

I beam at our Eldest One. I am made in his image, but I never knew it until tonight.

"Before I was born, my face was my grandfather's."

Ayame clicks her tongue, unimpressed. "Any mirror could tell you that," she says. "You've always looked like him."

After supper Grandfather and Sensei retire to the tearoom to drink another cup. Through the rice-paper wall, we can see them huddled together, heads almost touching.

When Yoshi gestures to the partially closed screen, we don't hesitate. Sensei told us that samurai kids need to be good listeners, and he's always telling us to do more practice.

Through the rice-paper wall, we can see them huddled together, heads almost touching.

"Which way does the wind blow, old friend?" Sensei asks.

"Is your grandfather a ninja?" whispers Taji.

I shake my head. "Of course not. He couldn't sneak past a rock."

"The wind blows many ways," Grandfather replies. "The Dragon Master has not reached the castle, but your friends are already inside."

What friends? We thought Sensei had only enemies waiting for him.

"The streets of Toyozawa are filled with rumors of your return. I have whispered many myself. The Emperor is expecting you to appear any day now. But even more important than that, what happened in Hell Valley? Did the ghosts give you any advice?"

"Not this time. I must try to wait patiently until they are ready to help me. They chose to speak to Niya with a message about using one slipper," says Sensei. "I'm glad you wrote to me about your grandson. The Dragon Master was a fool not to accept him as a student."

"Dragons have big, fast wings but small, slow brains. No wonder I never fit in when I studied there." Grandfather chuckles. "Buddha taught that we are born as Cockroaches so we can work our way up to being reborn as Dragons. Just goes to show that no one is right all the time."

It's a good joke, but Sensei doesn't laugh. "I, too, make mistakes," he says sadly.

Grandfather's voice softens. "It is the way of the Tao. There cannot be light without dark. There cannot be good without evil. Not even in one man."

"Who is he talking about?" Kyoko whispers.

"Maybe it's the Emperor," says Yoshi.

"Or the Dragon Master," Nezume suggests.

Or Sensei. Our teacher is wise and kind, but what if he really *did* do something evil? Good and evil in one man. It's the perfect description of a *tengu* goblin priest. Why else would Sensei need advice from the ghosts of Hell Valley?

The door slides open, but this time we're not ashamed to be caught.

"We are practicing gathering information," announces Yoshi.

"Excellent. Then I do not need to repeat anything," Sensei says. "But now it is time for your ears to sleep. Good night, Little Cockroaches."

I lead the way to my room, where Mother has laid seven mats on the floor.

"Your sister is very beautiful," says Nezume. "Like the moonflower."

Mikko sighs. "Like a lotus blossom."

"And what am I?" Kyoko asks. "Bamboo grass?"

Remembering Kyoko and the crane, I know it's important to say the right thing. I want to tell her how beautiful she is, but once again, I can't find any words.

Luckily, Yoshi knows what to say. "You are *yukika*. The snow flower."

"Not an ugly snow monkey?" There's a smile in her voice now.

Taji leans over to give her a hug. "Snow monkeys are cuddly."

"So why doesn't anyone make eyes at me?" she demands.

It's a challenge that answers itself. She would beat us up if we did.

"You are our sister," Yoshi says. "We look at you and we feel proud."

I keep my mouth shut. I know how I feel when I look at my sister. And it doesn't feel at all like that when I look at Kyoko.

CHAPTER EIGHT

真

THE CASTLE
WALLS

At sunrise we take our leave. We will travel along the main road now. There's no need for secrecy anymore. No one would dare harm those whom the Emperor is expecting.

But none of that matters if we can't convince the Emperor to stop the drum before the war begins. And if Sensei loses his head first, he won't even get a chance to speak. What will we do then?

I know what Sensei would say. "We will worry about that when we get there. Why waste time on what might never be?"

I try, but I can't stop worrying.

"You should reach the east gate by midday," says Father.

My grandfather grins. "Ki-Yaga doesn't need a gate."

"Sensei's going to fly over the walls," Mikko murmurs, elbowing me in the ribs.

I'd like to poke him back, but Father is watching and he wouldn't approve. The White Crane lifts its head high, ignoring the lizard at its foot.

I'm the last to say good-bye, lingering for one final kiss from Mother and a hug from Ayame. The men in my family are more reserved. But when Father and

Grandfather gaze at me with pride, it feels just like another hug.

Beside me Mikko dawdles with a whispered message for my sister. "I'll be back with a bag full of gold. And a writing brush. Just you wait."

She answers softly, "I think I will."

Now I can tease Mikko. I'll poke *him* in the ribs this time and clutch theatrically at my heart. But if he did marry Ayame one day, we'd be related. The laughter bubbling in my throat drains away. I think I'll help him fill that bag with gold.

"Chop, chop, Little Cockroaches," Sensei calls to us.

Grandfather raises a hand in farewell, his fingers stained with black smudges. He likes to play with fireworks, and once he set the roof ablaze. But I'll never think of him as doddery ever again. I saw the respect in Sensei's eyes, and I heard him ask Grandfather for advice.

This morning other people share the road around the edge of town. Women with straw baskets on their backs and children on their hips. Men going to work in the fields. The occasional ox and one barking dog that follows us until Sensei waves his staff and growls.

"I liked your family." Kyoko sighs. "I wish I had one like it."

"The Cockroach Ryu is a family," says Sensei. "You have more brothers than any sister should have to put up with."

"That's true." She laughs. "What about you, Sensei? Do you have any brothers or sisters?"

It's hard to imagine Sensei as a young boy, wrestling with a brother or pulling a sister's hair.

"I had a sister once. She's dead now."

That's sad but not surprising. Sensei is very old, and his sister would be old, too. We wait for Sensei to tell us about her. There's usually a story, but not this time.

The silence is interrupted by two women arguing on the roadside. One yells, waving a plum in the other's face. The second shouts, brandishing a peach. If fruit was a weapon, both women would be in slices.

"Old, wise one," they call to Sensei. "Help us, please."

Sensei bows low. "How may I assist?"

"I say a plum is worth more than a peach," declares the first woman, handing Sensei a plum.

"I say a peach is worth more than a plum." The second places a large yellow fruit in Sensei's other hand.

Before Sensei can speak, they begin arguing again.

Sensei drops both pieces of fruit in the dirt, grinding them into dusty pulp with his sandals. No longer bickering, the women stand openmouthed. Sensei has worked his first piece of magic. He has made them stop and listen.

"If you do not want each other's fruit, then neither has value. But if you do, one is not better than the other. You must trade with honor."

Bowing to Sensei's wisdom, the women fill his arms with fruit. We continue on our way with sticky peach fingers and red plum-juice mouths. Sensei was right, of course. One is not better than the other.

The road echoes with the stomp of marching feet. A procession is coming. *Thump. Thump. Ta-thum. Thump.* A drum beats loud and insistent, in ominous time with the one in my head. "Come look," it pounds. "Hear my noise. See how important my travelers are." As the group draws nearer, red and gold banners flash against the sun. Their master swaggers in front.

Nezume gasps.

It's the Dragon Master. He holds his head high and is oblivious to the dust and traffic around him. Six of his

It's the Dragon Master.

students follow with bags, weapons, and boxes of all sizes. They are big and strong and carry the load effortlessly. Their faces echo their master's haughty disdain.

People stop to stare. The tallest Dragon boy raises his sword high, and the crowd cheers.

Sensei shakes his head. "A sword is not a flag to be waved in the wind."

The crowd roars again.

"Some people are easily fooled," says Sensei. "All that glitters is not gold. Sometimes it is just shiny rubbish."

The procession is almost out of sight now. The arrogant master and his students didn't even notice us. Perhaps it was best the Dragon Master didn't lower his gaze to meet Sensei's eyes. Imagine the sparks then. The grass would be burning.

Ta-thum. Thum-thum. Thump. The drum is only an echo, but its message is loud and clear. Six days to war.

Yoshi sighs. "Their uniforms *were* splendid."

I don't like to admit it, but he's right. Our drab brown robes are covered with dust and splattered with mud.

"Did you see all the feathers on the Dragon Master's helmet?" asks Nezume.

He wants one like it, and so do I. Our bare heads are thick with grit from the road.

"Did you see the size of the broadsword the last kid was carrying?" I ask.

It's hard not to be impressed.

Sensei thumps his staff on the ground to call us to attention. "Weapons should be avoided wherever possible. Or chosen carefully for the task. Size does not matter. Would you use a hatchet to remove a fly from the face of a friend?"

I grin. "I might if it was Mikko bugging me."

"If there was a fly buzzing around, it wouldn't be on my forehead. It would be on your smelly slipper," he retorts.

I swipe at him, and he dodges, laughing, just out of reach.

Giving in to temptation, I take off my slipper and throw it.

The others prefer to walk in sandals. But sometimes, when we have been traveling a long time, I find my slipper more comfortable.

"Perhaps we should leave Niya's slipper alone." Sensei's eyes twinkle as he hands it back to me. "The spirit messenger said it is fated for great things. But right now, it is destined to walk some more."

Sandals and slipper slap against the road. Nobody notices *our* little procession. Outwardly, there is nothing golden about us. Sensei teaches us to shine inside.

"The Dragon Master will get to the castle first," Nezume says. "What if he turns the Emperor against us?"

Sensei shakes his head. "At the castle, there are many procedures and protocols. The Emperor must set an example by following his own rules. He will wait for us. And besides, it is bad manners not to do so. Even the Son of Heaven does not want to be in trouble with his teacher."

What about the Emperor's decree that if Sensei returns he must forfeit his head? There's nothing polite about that. I've always hated rules. Now more than ever.

But Sensei doesn't seem worried about the future of his head. He leaves that to me. We walk along, kicking dust in the Dragon Master's footprints. Sensei whistles, tapping the ground with his staff. He nods politely to a fat man with a mat under his arm and calls a greeting to a farmer working in a field beside the road.

Father was right. By midday we have reached the

castle wall. And Grandfather was right, too. There's not a gate to be seen.

The wall stretches high to tug the clouds into place around its turrets and towers. Along the base of the wall runs a moat. We stop underneath a giant cherry tree. But Sensei's usual space in the shade is already taken by a large dirty man, asleep in the ragged remains of a red kimono and jacket — snoring there without his trousers on. We don't know which way to look. Sensei makes it even harder when he sits down next to the tramp.

"Wake up," he bellows into the man's ear. "Lunch has arrived."

Seaweed-green eyes snap open. "Good." The tramp smiles at Sensei. "I haven't eaten for three days. I am hungry enough to eat my bamboo hat."

I can't see a hat anywhere. Maybe he's eaten it already.

Dutifully, we unroll the lunch Mother packed and spread it on the grass. Sensei's new friend eats so fast, even Yoshi has trouble keeping up.

Leaning back against the tree, the big man burps loudly and looks up the wall. "It's a long way to the top."

"Always is," Sensei agrees.

Like a flea-riddled dog, the tramp scratches his ear so hard, his knees shake. I shift a little to the left so any dislodged fleas don't jump onto me. Cockroaches and fleas don't get along at all.

"Are you going in tonight?" the tramp asks.

"As soon as it's dark," replies Sensei. "I have business to complete before I let the Emperor know we have arrived."

We look up at the wall, amazed. The swim across the moat would be freezing cold, but the climb is impossible.

"How are we going to get over that wall?" Nezume shakes his head.

Maybe the Snow Monkey could scale it, but the rest of us haven't got a chance. Unless Sensei really can work a little magic.

The wizard smiles and waves his bamboo wand. "I have arranged for some expert help."

"Who?" we chorus.

The tramp bursts into a spasm of guffaws, spattering bits of rice all over Yoshi. Politely, Yoshi wipes the food spittle from his jacket and his cheek.

"Only a ninja can climb a wall like that," the tramp

says. "What are you teaching these students, Master, that they don't know such obvious things?"

Sensei sighs. "They are still learning to listen. I have taught them Nothing, and it is all they know."

The tramp burps again. "Nothing is enough, Master."

Sensei rummages in his pack and pulls out a pair of trousers. They must have belonged to Onaku. Sensei's skinny pants would never fit this huge man. How did Sensei know to bring Onaku's trousers?

Fully clothed, the tramp nods his thanks before closing his eyes to sleep and snore again.

"Who is he?" Kyoko whispers.

"A *ronin*," says Sensei. "A wandering samurai who serves no lord but chooses to travel his own path. A lot like us."

Mikko gently lifts the *ronin*'s jacket. "Phew. It wouldn't take a ninja to smell this vagabond coming. If he's a warrior, where's his sword? All he has is a student's wooden *bokken*."

Taji wrinkles his nose. "Perhaps he lost his samurai sword."

It's almost unimaginable. But if anyone could do it, it would be this scruffy man.

"Maybe he is not deserving enough," Nezume suggests.

Sensei's eyes dance. "Perhaps he does not need one. He might be a better swordsman than any of us."

Not likely. This man is no skilled samurai. He's not even a worthy opponent. Mikko could easily beat him one-handed. Even on one leg, I'm sure I could too.

"All that glitters is not gold," Sensei reminds us. "And all that smells is not rubbish."

While we play games to pass the time, Sensei joins the *ronin* in a snoring bout. Sensei is a champion snorer, but it's a close competition and we quickly lose interest in judging it. Kyoko draws a grid in the dirt. I'm an expert at hopping games. Throwing a stone, we jump from square to square, avoiding the lines. It's good practice for getting across the mats to the tea ceremony.

Late in the afternoon, Sensei wakes. With his staff he raps our new companion across the knees.

"Dinner?" the *ronin* asks hopefully.

Kyoko lays out the remains of our food and we race our guest to the last honey cake.

The *ronin* belches appreciatively. "Now I will tell you a story in return for your hospitality. Would you like to hear what happened to my trousers?"

We nod, shifting ourselves into a storytelling circle. The White Crane bends closer. It loves a good story.

"Listen and learn, young samurai. I am about to tell you a tale of great strategy."

Losing your trousers doesn't sound like much of a strategy to me.

"On the way to the castle, I was challenged by a renowned swordsman, victorious in his last fifteen duels. I did not want to hurt such an esteemed opponent."

It's hard to imagine his opponent was in any danger. Kyoko swallows a giggle and Sensei glares, but the *ronin* doesn't notice. Like all good stories, this one has a life of its own. It doesn't need to feed off the faces of its listeners.

"I required a strategy to disorientate my opponent. Something to make him hesitate."

"Because he who hesitates has already lost," Taji says.

The *ronin* chuckles, scratching the stray whiskers on his chin. "It seems your students have been listening, Master. To distract my worthy adversary, I decided to take off my trousers."

That's not so silly after all. It's enough to make anyone stop and stare.

"My opponent refused to fight someone he thought was an idiot. He went away. So I notched a victory on my scabbard, and my respected foe survived unharmed. But no plan is perfect, and while I was congratulating myself, a gust of wind blew my trousers into the nearby lake. They sleep with the sweetfish now."

"Your opponent was very fortunate. It was his lucky day," Sensei says.

What? Sensei thinks this ruffian would have won? He's got to be kidding.

"My lucky day, too. I didn't need my pants or my sword that morning," the *ronin* says. "Sometimes it is not what you have but what you don't have. So I gave my sword away to someone who needed it more."

That sounds like something Sensei would teach. And Sensei is nodding, pleased, as if he was somehow involved.

"Everything is not as it looks," he says. "The easiest opponent is the one who thinks he has already won."

Like the Dragon Master?

Sensei nods inside my head. I'm getting used to it now.

"I wouldn't mind fighting if I didn't have to use a sword or hurt anyone," Yoshi says.

"As long as you keep your trousers on. We don't need your lumpy legs to look at," teases Mikko.

"Sometimes it is good to be blind." Taji laughs. "There are some things no one should have to see."

Bellies full, Sensei and the *ronin* are soon snoring again. We wait excitedly for the adventure that tonight promises. Just a few hours to go, but the time crawls like a caterpillar.

"What if this tattered tramp really is a famous swordsman?" I whisper.

Nezume shrugs. "Like who?"

"Sensei seems to know him. He might even be Mitsuka Manuyoto."

The others giggle and guffaw, Mikko loudest of all.

"You think Sensei is a *tengu* and some old vagabond is the celebrated swordsman Manuyoto. A national hero who saved the Emperor from even more assassins than Sensei? Sometimes, Niya, you have mung beans for brains."

My friends laugh even louder, waking Sensei and the *ronin*.

"*Mmmh.*" The *ronin* yawns. "Is there any leftover supper?"

"Eating must wait. There is work to do." Sensei rises, shaking his long, skinny arms. He stretches his legs and touches his toes.

The *ronin* lumbers to his feet, looks down, and decides to stay upright.

Long, deep shadows have draped across the castle town. An owl hoots. A bat screeches. Night clambers over the walls and just behind it, a small dark figure.

CHAPTER NINE

仁

THE OWL HOOTS

Darkness chases the ninja down the wall. We strain to see his shadow disappear against the night. We struggle to listen. But all we hear is the muffled *bok-bok* of frogs in the weeds. Not a ripple breaks the water until the ninja emerges to shake himself like a wet cat. He runs toward us on silent feline feet.

Bowing low, he doesn't rise until Sensei taps him on the shoulder.

"Master," the small but familiar voice says.

Before I can fit the words to a face, the sword on the ninja's belt calls out to me. Izuru, the blade of my childhood.

Last year, I gave it to the young village boy who was carried to the *ryu* with a broken leg. While Sensei straightened the bone, the boy bit hard on the hilt of my sword. Once his teeth marks were on the leather, I knew where Izuru belonged. I was ready to wear the *katana* and *wakizashi* of the warrior samurai, and it was time to let Izuru go.

I know I did the right thing. I can hear it in Izuru's song.

The boy turns to me. Up close, in the gray gloom, I can see him clearly. He's wearing a dark indigo-blue suit, the night uniform of the ninja. His body and face are covered except for his hands and a narrow slit across his eyes so he can see.

Taji has recognized the voice, too. A voice is like a face in his memory.

"Hello, Riaze," he says.

"Hello, Little Cockroaches." Riaze bows to each of us in turn, including the *ronin*.

We all bow our response. It's a well-coordinated movement, perfectly timed to avoid a lot of head knocking and forehead rubbing. We learned this the hard way. The first time we bowed together, I received a lump the size of a duck egg. And Mikko had one even bigger.

Riaze touches the sword at his side. "I am taking good care of Izuru. I have not drawn it once in a fight. But I have taken it out of the scabbard many times to admire the blade and listen to its song."

"Thank you," I say, bending as deeply as I can.

Some things are really important, and this is one of them. A samurai kid never forgets his first sword. Even when he grows old enough to carry a longer, sharper blade by his side, he still keeps the memory of his first sword in his heart.

"Why didn't you return to the *ryu* to study with us?" asks Kyoko.

"I was greatly honored when Ki-Yaga offered to instruct me, but I was called elsewhere." Riaze grins. "It seems Sensei has come to teach me anyway. Before he begins, I must do some teaching of my own."

Riaze unstraps a bag from his back. Crouching, he empties the contents onto the ground and we drop to our haunches beside him.

First, he hands each of us a ninja-blue jacket and baggy trousers.

"Put these over your clothes. Brown is easy to see in the shadows, but blue will make you invisible."

Now the *ronin* has two pairs of trousers when this afternoon he had none.

"Are you coming with us?" Yoshi asks him.

"I wouldn't miss this for anything. Why else would I wait around for three days outside the castle wall?" His teeth gleam bright through the shadows.

"You are much appreciated," says Sensei. "We need all the help we can gather."

The *ronin* bows. "It is always an honor to wait for you, Teacher."

"That's not what you used to say." Sensei laughs. "I believe you once called me a slow old turtle, and I had to chase you with a stick to prove it wasn't true."

It's hard to imagine Sensei chasing this great bear around. Before we can ask for the whole story, Riaze holds up a metal bar with straps and spikes.

"With these ninja climbing claws on your hands and feet, you will be able to scale the wall like monkeys." He winks at Kyoko.

Kyoko slips a hand claw on, adjusting the straps and making room for her extra finger.

"Have you worn these before?" Nezume asks.

She shakes her head, flexing her knuckles. "It's easy to see how they go."

Not for me. I turn the metal band over and over. It won't fit my hand at all.

"That's a foot claw," says Riaze. "I'll show you how to put it on."

My leg is soon a lethal weapon, metal prongs protruding from the bottom of my toes. I imagine kicking an opponent. I wouldn't need two feet to fight if I had a spiky slipper.

Not a bad idea, for a ninja, Sensei teases inside my head.

I'm used to hearing his voice there now, and I like it. It's a special bond between us.

Before I have one handpiece in place, Sensei is ready. He's worn this climbing equipment before! And so has the *ronin.* He's already dressed and helping Taji with the buckles.

From the smaller bag hanging on his belt, Riaze removes a bundle of bamboo tubes. He gives us one each.

"We'll use these to cross the moat underwater. For many months my ninja clan has been piling stones in the ditch here to build a ridge across the bottom. If we walk along it, the water will flow just above our heads."

Riaze demonstrates how to use the bamboo tubes. "One end of the tube goes in your mouth, and the other sits above the waterline. If any water splashes into the tube, blow hard and it will clear."

Now I know why Sensei came to this section of the wall. And I know it's not coincidence that the *ronin* was waiting in the same place. They came to meet at the underwater bridge.

"This is how the ninja move across a river unseen. We do not splash and splutter like the swimming samurai." Riaze chuckles.

"I thought the ninja could walk *on* water," Taji says.

I've heard that, too. My father believes they have special shoes that glide across the surface, as if by magic. My grandfather says it is a good story and repeats it whenever he can.

Riaze laughs even louder. "That's just a myth. But words are powerful weapons. With each telling of the story, our imagined supernatural powers grow more believable. It's easy to fool a superstitious man, even a samurai or an emperor. Some men think we can vanish into thin air."

That sounds reasonable to me. Riaze disappeared when he was climbing down the wall. I saw it with my own eyes.

"It is hard to fight or track an opponent you can't see," Taji agrees. "You have to listen very hard."

The *ronin* slaps his hand against his leg. "I don't like listening anytime. If you can't beat them, join them, I say."

"Is that what we're doing, Sensei?" Yoshi asks.

Our teacher nods. "The way of the warrior has many paths to be walked many different ways. To silence the war drum, we must also creep on ninja feet."

Or in my case, hop on a ninja foot. Preferably with spikes on it.

"I will walk in samurai sandals," says Riaze. "I'm proud to carry Izuru by my side, and all my friends are envious. No ninja weapon compares to a samurai sword."

Sensei was right. We have much to learn from one another. We won the Annual Trainee Games because we worked together as a team. Inside the castle wall, a greater challenge is waiting. We must convince the Emperor to stop the war before he chops off Sensei's head. But this time our team is even stronger. We have two new members. Izuru chose Riaze many months ago, and I suspect Sensei chose the *ronin* long before that.

Riaze is looking in his belt bag again. Ninja might not wear magic shoes, but the bags they carry are full of tricks. What else could he possibly have in there?

He extracts a small bamboo cylinder. "You will like this best of all."

"What's it do?" Kyoko asks.

"It warms your heart. More than any kiss ever will."

As Kyoko reaches to take the cylinder, Riaze brushes her clawed hand against his lips.

Kyoko giggles, and my glare slices through the darkness between them.

"The tube *is* warm," she says, surprised.

"We pack embers inside layers of bamboo. It will generate heat for hours," Riaze promises. "And it's useful if you want to burn down a building."

The ninja use fire to flush out their victims. Father once said that a ninja can shoot flames from the palm of his hand. But Grandfather said, "All fires begin with a little spark. There's no magic in that." He knew about the ember cylinders. I should have paid more attention to Grandfather's stories. For years his wisdom was right under my nose and I never once breathed it in.

"There is a waterproof pocket inside your jacket," Riaze informs us.

I place the cylinder in it carefully. Warmth spreads through the pocket, across my chest.

But Mikko has other worries on his mind than being wet and cold. He's looking up anxiously. "It's very high."

"But not as difficult as it looks," Sensei reassures us. "The wall is pitted with handholds."

How does he know that? Maybe he can fly.

Or maybe he's climbed it before.

"I have left a grappling hook at the top of the wall. It's holding a rope ladder you can use," says Riaze. "Stick close and flat against the wall. We call it lizard walking."

Our Striped Gecko doesn't look convinced.

"Don't worry, Mikko. The ladder will help you climb like a ninja." When Riaze came to the *ryu,* it was Mikko who held his hand and made him laugh to forget the pain. Now it is Riaze's turn to help.

"You'll be all right," Nezume says, belting Mikko on the shoulder. "One arm never bothered you before. And it won't this time."

Mikko shakes his head. "It's not that." He pauses. "I'm afraid of heights."

"But you stand on the edge of our mountain looking into the valley," says Kyoko. "It makes me dizzy to watch."

"That's different. I feel safe because we're all standing there. I know Yoshi would reach out and grab me."

"Then I'll go last," says Yoshi. "And if you slip, I'll catch you."

Kyoko giggles. "Squashed Yoshi."

"The biggest problem is owls," Sensei says. "They

have nests all over the wall and their beaks are sharp. If you put your finger in the wrong place, you might lose it."

"I've got a spare finger, anyway." Kyoko shrugs.

The White Crane isn't scared of other birds either.

"I heard an owl calling earlier," says Taji. "I listened hard but I couldn't hear its wings."

"That's because it was me." Riaze puffs with pride. "I am a member of the Owl Ninja Clan. *Tu-whit. Tu-whoo.*" He hoots, soft and familiar, into the night.

In my memory an owl answers. Grandfather's tearoom scroll. The Crane, the Bat, the Lizard, the Tiger, the Rat, the Monkey. And the Owl. It's not Sensei at all. It's Riaze. Was Grandfather sending me a message?

"Time to go," the *ronin* reminds us. "We need to reach the Owl Dojo before midnight."

It's easy to walk with a claw on my foot. We follow Riaze into the moat, gasping as the icy water clutches our throats. It crushes against my chest until the fire in my pocket forces it to let go. I hop as fast as I can.

The ridge across the bottom is narrow and uneven. I concentrate carefully. My thoughts hold my mind in place, but my foot slips. Cold water fills my breathing tube. I am gasping and sputtering; the world around me turns to bubbles. I want to scream, but I force myself not to panic. A boy who has faced a ghost is not afraid of drowning. It's like I'm dreaming—I see the world through Taji's eyes, all gray and black.

Om-om, Sensei says inside my head. My waterlogged brain struggles to stay awake. *Om-om,* I force myself to answer.

The *ronin's* strong bear arms lift me back onto the ridge. I try not to gulp as I blow out to clear the tube. My aching lungs stretch and snap back into shape. My friends are ahead of me and don't even know what has happened. I'll have a good story to tell tonight at the dojo.

Riaze and Sensei reach the wall first. Sensei climbs like a spindly-legged garden spider. Kyoko follows quickly, but Riaze stops to help Mikko onto the first rung of the ladder. I'm just behind Nezume, Taji, and Yoshi. And the *ronin.* Like a column of ants, we scrape a trail up the wall.

Sensei is first to the top. His arms are skinny but strong—thin strands of unbreakable bamboo. The *ronin* is last. His arms are short but strong—bolts of bamboo

Sensei is first to the top.

matting. Climbing is all about arms, and I've got two of those. But it's hard with only one foot to rest against.

Like a sky ninja, the pale moon creeps from behind the clouds. I can see all the way to the castle keep. In the middle of the compound stands the main building where the Emperor sleeps. Four smaller buildings surround it, connected by passageways. Somewhere inside, Sensei will confront the Emperor and speak out against the drum.

The White Crane likes it up here. It shakes its feathers, itching to fly.

"Someone's coming," Taji whispers.

"Which direction?" asks Riaze.

"East."

"Everyone flat against the top of the wall." Dropping quickly, Riaze shows us how.

Crunch. Crunch. Crunch. The sound of samurai boots draws closer. The White Crane huddles paralyzed with fear, and the goldfish in my stomach hold their breath. *Ta-thum. Thum-thump.* My heart beats a reminder: six days to war.

Directly below me, two soldiers stop to argue. They smell as if they've been drenched in *sake* and rolled in warm mouse droppings. It's worse than the sulfur steam of Hell Valley.

In front of me, Nezume wriggles. He's not good at keeping still. He's usually the first to move when we practice statues.

Tsst. A small stone drops to the ground. *Tsst.* Another follows.

"What was that?" the first soldier asks.

"I didn't hear anything."

The first soldier looks along the wall. "I heard something. We should check."

"Do it yourself, Jungo. I'm not listening to you anymore. That's how I got into this trouble in the first place," the second soldier grumbles. "If you hadn't convinced me to gamble against the captain, we'd be home drinking hot *sake* instead of doing extra guard duty."

"Shh. Stop whining, Shouji, and let me listen," Jungo says.

"It was probably an owl. The place is riddled with the scraggly, stinking things."

"Tu-whit. Tu-whoo," Riaze hoots in protest.

"Hear that? What did I tell you, noodle-head? The

only thing threatening to attack the castle has claws and feathers," says Shouji.

Riaze rustles in his belt bag. It's a sound as soft as owl wings, but I'm a good listener.

Ssst. Pfft. A white cloud of smoke balloons to envelop us all. Another ninja trick.

"This ocean mist is thicker than day-old miso soup. Do you still want to go owl hunting?" Shouji sneers.

"Nah. I suppose you're right."

The two soldiers grumble their way into a farther corner of the night.

"Ninja are always pleased to see the castle defenses in the safe hands of the samurai," Riaze taunts. "It makes our job easier."

The *ronin's* teeth flash a grin into the darkness, and Sensei snorts in mock indignation.

"It would be different if it was me. I could do it one-handed," Mikko boasts.

He'd have to. It's all he's got. But he wouldn't be doing it alone. The Cockroach Ryu is a team. We stick together like rice and honey.

After Riaze is sure the soldiers have left, he hauls the rope ladder up and drops it down the other side. As we near the ground, a ghostly-white shadow swoops low over our heads. Somewhere nearby, a mouse squeals.

"The owl strikes, silent and deadly," Sensei says, dropping expertly to the ground.

Yoshi lands on all fours, like a cat. I collapse with a thump to provide a soft cushion for Mikko, who lands on top of me. There's nothing graceful about our entrance, but only the moon is watching. It winks and returns to hide behind the clouds.

"Keep the climbing claws," says Riaze. "You might need them again one day."

Mikko won't like it if we do. And I would rather fly.

We edge along the dark shadowed streets, around corners, through narrow gateways. Around and around, until I'm hopelessly lost.

"*Yeow*. I stepped on a rock," Yoshi whispers through clenched teeth. "I can't see a thing."

"Me neither. How am *I* expected to find my way?" Taji laughs.

"The road is curved so that even in daylight attackers cannot see very far ahead," says Sensei. "But now that you are trainee ninja, you don't need eyes to see where you must go. More practice, Little Cockroaches.

Tomorrow your training begins at the Owl Dojo. We have many challenges ahead, and you will need new skills to meet them."

Oh, no. Back to school.

Mikko groans, and the *ronin* laughs.

Pressing his fingers against his lips, Riaze leads us through the maze to a small wooden entrance.

Yoshi reads the words above the door: "Kitchen staff."

"The best place for a ninja clan to hide is under the Emperor's nose," Sensei says approvingly.

"Owl Ninja are also the castle kitchen hands. My miso soup will make your mouth water," Riaze brags.

"Tu-whoo, tu-whoo," he calls softly.

The door creaks open. Just wide enough for the face behind it to see what the owl has dragged in. Just enough for the smell to reach out and tug at our tastebuds.

Hot miso soup. *Mmmm.* I can't help it. Drool pools in the corners of my mouth.

CHAPTER TEN

名誉

INSIDE THE
OWL DOJO

Last night was a tired blur of welcoming smiles, my tale of almost drowning, a hot bath, and the best miso soup ever. This morning I'm hungry again and hoping for another bowl.

In the dojo dining room, we are quickly surrounded by familiar faces from our mountain village. One of them makes the hair on the back of my neck bristle. It is the face of a dead man. Black eyes lurk behind shaggy eyebrows. Gray furry hair covers his chin and cheeks. His mouth curls, almost into a snarl. I'd never forget a face like that.

We accompanied Sensei to his funeral two years ago. Women howled, banging their rice cooking pots. The bright red coffin was lowered into the fire, and that night we sent a flotilla of lanterns down the river. Without a proper farewell, a soul wanders for eternity — like the ghosts of Hell Valley. But everything was done right for this man. Why can't his spirit rest in peace?

Goose bumps crawl across my chest as the ghost's wolf-like stare hunts me down. But then he grins, and there are no pointed rows of teeth — just a smile.

"Your face is pale, young Cockroach. I am surprised you remember my mock funeral."

"Niya has a memory like a steel boar trap and the fastest brain on any number of legs." Sensei beams proudly.

My goose bumps are gone now. I pretend they were never there at all.

"I'm used to talking with *real* ghosts," I brag. Yoshi stomps on my foot, reminding me to be polite, but I continue. "When we passed through Hell Valley, a ghost chose to speak with *me*."

"Then I am pleased to have such a famous person in my dojo," the man says with a chuckle.

The wolf man is the Ninja Master! I wish I'd listened to Yoshi's stomp.

I bow, low and humble. "I meant no disrespect. It was only half a ghost, not very frightening at all."

The Ninja Master nods, pardoning my insolence. "When I was chosen as clan leader, I had to disappear from my old life. Death is the ultimate vanishing act."

Ninja are famous for their tricks, and this master is a great magician.

His hypnotic stare binds me tight, piercing deep into my heart. The White Crane looks into the Wolf's eyes, unafraid.

Satisfied with what he finds, the Wolf releases us both.

"I am honored to have Ki-Yaga return to the Owl Dojo. It will be a privilege to teach his students."

I know I can trust this man. He could have swallowed my soul, but he chose not to. And there's something more: I recognize the wolf Yoshi and I saw on the mountain track just before the earthquake that almost killed me. Even then, the ninja were watching over us.

The Ninja Master places his hand on my shoulder. "Let us share breakfast and after that"—he laughs— "more practice."

Sensei nods his approval, but my friends and I groan. Around us, the Owl Ninja trainees echo our opinion. Ninja and samurai are not so different after all.

We're lucky the ninja of the Owl Dojo work as castle kitchen staff. They cook a wonderful breakfast.

"Never eat a big meal before a battle," Sensei taught us. "Sometimes in combat, a samurai sees things that make him glad his stomach is empty."

But we're only training today, so we pile our plates high.

"This is the best fish I've ever eaten," says Taji.

Yoshi belches. "These are the best *three* fish I've ever eaten."

We all murmur appreciatively, except the *ronin*. His goldfish cheeks are stuffed too full to make any noise.

After more breakfast than I've ever eaten before, an elderly ninja leads us in meditation and warm-up exercises.

"How can he teach us?" Kyoko whispers. "He's so old. If he stretches anything, it will snap in two."

Coughing softly, Sensei reminds us to be respectful or his old arms will teach us a lesson with his traveling staff.

A ninja needs to be flexible. Limb by limb, we stretch everything. By the time we've finished, I feel twice as tall as before.

The Ninja Master arrives to watch our progress. "Today each Cockroach student will learn a different skill," he announces. "Then, together, you will be expert at them all."

We're used to that. We have never been expert at anything on our own. Blind eyes, one leg, one arm. But our team is strong, with many arms and legs, able to see in the dark.

"Ki-Yaga and I have agreed on what each trainee needs to know. Yoshi will study concealment and disguise, learning to transform into other things and other people."

"He's going to be a ninja rock," Mikko teases.

Yoshi growls gently. "Kick me and you'll be sorry."

We laugh, but it's an excellent choice. Yoshi is already a rock. We lean on him all the time.

"Taji will learn espionage. Ninja have ways of listening that the samurai have never heard of," the master says. "Kyoko will train in the garden with our women."

Dark clouds thunder across Kyoko's face. "I'm just as good as the boys." She glowers, eyes flashing like lightning.

"The master did not say any different," Sensei intercedes. "You might be surprised at what you learn. If you leave your mind open, anything can fly in."

I always try to keep my mind open wide. Maybe *that's* how Sensei flies in so easily.

"A girl who can fight like a boy is the perfect surprise weapon," the Ninja Master says. "She will make the warrior hesitate and . . ."

"He who hesitates has already lost," we all chorus, including the *ronin*.

"You have taught your students well, Ki-Yaga."

Sensei nods, pleased with us and with the Ninja Master's praise.

"I will teach Nezume to fight with a ninja dagger, and Mikko will learn to use explosives. Niya will practice unarmed combat." The Wolf grins, sly but wise. "Maybe his slipper will learn new tricks."

Good. I grin, too. Then I'll be able to try those tricks out on Mikko.

Sensei eyes the cherry tree in the courtyard. "I think I will practice as well."

"I'll snore at your feet and learn from you," the *ronin* says. "It will be just like the old days."

We turn eagerly, hoping for the story. But somewhere a gong sounds, and we know what that means. No more chatter. Practice has begun.

"My name is Ako," my opponent says. He's smaller and thinner than me, but I'm not fooled by that. "I am also called Rice Boy," Ako continues, "because I make the best rice porridge in Toyozawa. And there is one more reason but I'll demonstrate that later."

I search his face for clues. But the ninja are masters of disguise. All I find is a smile.

Ako tucks one leg up and hops forward. He falls flat on his face but rises quickly, ready to hop again.

"Are you making fun of me?" I ask.

Ako looks offended. "A ninja would never insult a guest."

"Then why are you pretending to have one leg?"

"I want to fight like you. If I can manage on one leg, it doesn't matter if I fall and break an ankle."

I never thought about that before. What if I broke my ankle? The question answers itself. Yoshi and Mikko would argue about whose turn it was to carry me.

Ako and I begin to wrestle. Sometimes Ako wrestles me to the ground, and sometimes I topple him. But most of the time he stumbles and we crash together. It's not easy, but Ako refuses to give up, persisting until he can balance on one leg. Not as good as the White Crane but much better than Taji and Mikko.

"May I borrow your slipper?" he says. "I think it would be harder to fight with a shoe on."

"You are right," I agree, "but my slipper probably won't fit you."

It does. Perfectly. Now I have the advantage as my bare foot grips the floor.

We lock arms with a grunt.

Crash. Clunk.

We untangle legs with a giggle.

Riaze appears, raising his eyebrows at us. "Do you want to go and see what the others are doing?"

"We're supposed to practice wrestling," I say.

"We could practice stealth," suggests Ako. "All ninja have to learn that."

Riaze, Ako, and I sneak into the garden, where Kyoko is throwing *shuriken* stars. When Kyoko kicks me during unarmed fighting practice, I often see stars, but not like these. Each star has four razor-sharp points, and according to Grandfather's stories, sometimes they are dipped in poison.

At the far end of the garden, a woman stands holding a wooden pole. Kyoko swings her arm, and blades of metal spin across the open space to splinter the wood in the woman's hand. The woman doesn't flinch, but I do.

"What are you doing here?" Kyoko calls.

Riaze, Ako, and I sneak into the garden, where Kyoko is throwing *shuriken* stars.

I wave her over. "We're sneaking up on everyone."

"Come with us, and I'll show you how I broke my leg. You can try the climb," offers Riaze.

Kyoko can't resist a climbing challenge.

Riaze points to a thin bamboo string swinging high between two trees. *I'm not trying that,* I think. But Kyoko is already running toward the nearest trunk. She scrambles across on all fours and drops to the ground.

"Too easy. How could you possibly fall?"

"Hmph," Riaze snorts. "I'll show you."

He walks the string like a tightrope. Kyoko wants to try it that way, but black smoke is billowing from the hut at the other end of the garden. That's where Mikko is. We race to see what he's burning.

In the middle of the room, Mikko is filling an eggshell with dark powder.

"Look," he calls. "I'm mixing sand, pepper, and nettles. When I throw this in someone's eyes, they'll be blinder than Taji. Do you know what else I learned this morning?"

We shake our heads. I've never seen Mikko excited about learning anything.

"I can make a wall of flame, but I can't show you."

He grins sheepishly. "I burned a hole in the wall last time."

"Then you are almost as good as Grandfather," I say. "He set the roof on fire twice, and once he even singed his own beard."

"Has Mikko finished his lesson?" Ako asks the teacher.

The ninja nods, looking relieved that the instruction is over. Winking at me, Mikko slips the eggshells into his pocket, unnoticed by everyone else.

We're looking for Taji next, but he finds us first. He's finished learning to listen and is practicing with a bamboo cup against the dojo wall. "I heard you coming," he says, laughing. "But I didn't need the listening cup to hear Niya."

"You won't hear me anymore. Ako and Riaze are teaching me to creep like a ninja."

"I'll believe that when I hear it," Taji says.

The White Crane is learning to fly on owl wings, but the Golden Bat already knows how to swoop without a sound.

We need Taji's help to find Yoshi. He's sitting motionless, not making any noise at all. Yoshi has been practicing like this for years. Every day he sits on his rock overlooking the valley, thinking about the time years ago when he accidentally killed another boy. But ever since he shared the story, he doesn't spend as much time sitting alone.

"Would you like to see something dangerous?" Riaze asks. "It's in the next room."

We nod eagerly. Samurai kids race toward danger. Except when they don't know where they're going. The dojo is a maze of rice-paper walls, and they all look the same to me.

"There it is." Ako points to a raised platform in the middle of the room.

Why would a room need two floors? And what's so dangerous about that?

"This is a nightingale floor," Riaze says. "It sings."

"Like a sword?" Nezume asks.

When Riaze steps onto the wooden floor, the boards creak softly. "No. This is not a song you ever want to hear."

"Its notes are meant to rouse sleeping samurai guards," says Ako. He draws an imaginary sword across his neck. "One dead ninja."

"And if the samurai don't wake up?" Yoshi asks.

"One dead samurai," says the *ronin* from the doorway. Sensei, the Ninja Master, and Nezume are with him.

Are ninja and samurai enemies? Or friends?

You must decide for yourself, Sensei answers me.

"Even the Emperor now sleeps surrounded by a nightingale floor," says the Ninja Master. "We haven't yet found a way across."

Nezume turns, hand on his sword. "Do you want to kill the Emperor?"

"No. The Emperor is a good man, and I would defend his honor. But we must be prepared for the day when this floor lies between us and our enemy."

"A samurai doesn't like to sneak and kill," I say indignantly.

Riaze laughs. "That's why he hires a ninja to do it for him."

I'm about to argue, but Sensei and the *ronin* are nodding. *It's true!*

Yoshi steps onto the floor to stand beside Riaze. He has made his decision. And he's right. These ninja are our friends. One by one, we follow his lead until we're all standing in the middle of the floor and a flock of nightingales cries out in deadly song.

The sound is familiar, and the White Crane shakes its head, trying to remember. Sensei says that sometimes you need to tip your head sideways so you can look at a problem differently.

Or tip your ear so you can hear at a different angle.

Kyoko places her ear against the floor. "I know that sound."

Taking her *shakuhachi* flute from her pocket, she begins to play. Her six fingers play the bamboo flute until it sings in tune with the creaks and sighs of the floor.

When she stops playing, the Ninja Master bows low.

"I am in your debt," he says. "You will save many ninja lives."

The ninja are masters of deception, but they had nothing to hide behind when they stepped onto the nightingale floor. Now they can play Kyoko's song. Slumbering beneath the sound of a flute's lullabies, no one will hear the ninja creep.

We came here to end war in the mountains, and now beneath the castle wall we are ending another conflict, as samurai and ninja work together.

Sensei grins proudly. *I am such a good teacher.*

Yes, I answer. *And we are such good students.*

It's hard to listen when Sensei laughs inside my head. The Ninja Master is speaking again. "Let us celebrate by shouting," he says.

We shout to release *ki.* Sensei teaches us that *ki* is a powerful spiritual energy, stored in the stomach and more potent than one of Yoshi's belches. A great shout can startle an ambush or frighten an adversary. And it always feels good to yell.

"Yoh-oh-oh-oh," the Ninja Master's voice howls across the room. Nezume shivers, and Taji covers his ears.

Yoshi roars. The *ronin* growls. And the White Crane screeches. *Aye-ee-yah. Aye-ee-yah.*

Slowly, Sensei raises his arms. The room begins to quiver like an earthquake. The nightingale floor creaks and groans. Even the air trembles.

"Banzai!" he bellows.

When he lowers his arms, the world stills.

"That felt good," he says. "Now I am hungry enough to eat a horse."

He's lucky Uma didn't hear that!

After lunch our time is our own. But we know what we need to do. More ninja practice.

Sensei and the *ronin* are already practicing under the cherry tree again. I would like to learn to sleep and watch at the same time.

You will, Sensei whispers. *The skill is strong in your family.*

No, it's not. When Father sleeps, he doesn't hear a thing. Not even Ayame and me arguing. And we're louder than a throng of pitta birds.

Sensei shakes his head. He doesn't mean Father. *Who is always asleep in the corner?*

He means Grandfather!

"Come with me now. I will show you my special talent," Ako says. "Do you want to know why I am called Rice Boy?"

He leads us to a room where the floors shine with wax. "Watch this." He runs across the room, without slipping.

"You try," he dares us.

Nezume accepts the challenge first and lands on his backside. Mikko slides in behind him.

"I'm impressed, but what's that got to do with rice?" I call from the safety of the doorway.

Ako returns at full speed to stand beside me. Taking

a handful of rice from his pocket, he strews it over the floor. More slippery than ice! He runs across the room again, feet flying and skidding on the grains. But he doesn't even stumble. He makes it look easy.

But it's not. Riaze follows, almost making it to the middle before he drops with a thump. Yoshi slumps beside him, and Nezume tumbles on top of them both. The rest of us skid to form a heap of flailing arms and legs.

"*Yoh. Yah.*" Yelling, Ako launches himself on top of the pile. But we don't need to shout. The room is filled with the most powerful *ki* of all—friendship.

Nightfall is our signal to leave.

"I have a parting gift for each of you," the Ninja Master says.

Riaze and Ako step forward, their arms piled high with belts and daggers.

Once I would have sneered at ninja weaponry. But we have learned many things at the Owl Dojo, and one of those things is respect. The ninja blade might not sing like a sword, but it speaks powerful words of fellowship.

"We thank you, Master," Sensei says. "My students will keep your secrets safe."

The ninja have numerous places to hide their secrets—pockets filled with stars, knives in their boots, black powder in the end of their walking sticks, and scabbards with false bottoms. But a samurai uniform, with its layers of folds and wraps, has just as many perfect hiding places.

We bow low, proud to scrape our foreheads in the dust of the dojo floor.

"Return with honor, Little Cockroaches," the Ninja Master calls after us as we follow Sensei into the dark street.

Tu-whit. Tu-whoo.

"See you in the castle kitchen," Riaze says, hooting with soft laughter.

The air echoes with the noise of owls. And one lone wolf howl.

CHAPTER ELEVEN

忠誠

THE FIRST SCROLL

It's hard to sleep with all the shouting.

"Get up, old man!" the soldier bellows. "You can't lie here. You're blocking the castle keep gateway."

Sensei yawns, loud and wide. "Pardon?" There's nothing wrong with his ears. Ki-Yaga can hear a crane feather rustle, but sometimes he likes to pretend.

"Where did you come from? There's no record of you or your companions entering the main gate." The soldier grabs Sensei's traveling stick. That's not a good idea.

Slowly, the *ronin* opens one eye. He doesn't want to miss the fun.

Sensei's long, skinny leg strikes to trip the soldier.

Clump-fmp.

Standing, our teacher is suddenly taller, louder, and more frightening than the ogres in Grandfather's stories.

"I am Ki-Yaga. Master of the Cockroach Ryu. Former Imperial Teacher and Royal Bodyguard. The Emperor is expecting me, and while I do not expect much in return, I deserve better treatment than this."

Ki-Yaga's name has always opened doors. And now that it has been mentioned, the gates to the castle keep swing apart.

Kneeling, the soldier waits bare-necked for Sensei to draw his sword.

Instead, Sensei gently taps the man on the shoulder. "We all make mistakes," he says.

I want to ask Sensei about his mistake, but this isn't the time.

"My humble apologies, Sensei." On his feet again, the soldier takes charge. "We were instructed to watch for your arrival, but I did not expect to find you already inside the main gate." He barks an order, and guards rush to escort us through every gate between here and the Emperor's residence.

Beard flapping and cloak flying, Sensei strides between the soldiers. He's enjoying this! And so are we. The *ronin* puffs out his chest and swaggers, hand on his wooden sword. Kyoko giggles, waving to the people who line the streets and stare. If I had a drum, I would beat it proudly. *Ta-thum. Thum-thump.* We've come to stop the mountains from going to war.

At the entrance to the main building, a man is waiting. He wears a richly brocaded jacket and long baggy pants that drag across the floor. His snake-green eyes glitter with intelligence and authority. This is a man with an important job. Maybe the Emperor chose him especially to keep an eye on Sensei's head.

"Honored guests." The green-eyed court attendant bows. "The Emperor has asked me to greet you on his behalf. I will show you to your quarters. If there is anything you need, ring this bell to summon a servant boy."

He hands Sensei a gold bell. "Hot baths and clean clothes are waiting for you." His gaze slides down his nose to tell us our cockroach-brown traveling robes will not do here in the Emperor's compound.

We follow the attendant to a small building in the Imperial Garden.

"Breakfast will be delivered shortly. The castle has an excellent kitchen," our guide says.

We already know that. If I'm lucky, the meal will be Riaze's miso soup and Rice Boy's porridge.

The attendant's eyes narrow as he searches Sensei's face. "I have heard that you mysteriously appeared on the castle keep steps."

Sensei says nothing. The silent tension wraps itself around our throats. Mikko coughs, and the *ronin* scratches his neck.

Suspicious eyes drill even deeper. "Perhaps our guards were asleep or drunk when you passed through the main gate."

I don't like the sound of this. Someone could get into serious trouble. Maybe even lose a body part.

"Sir," I say, bowing low. "Do not punish the soldiers. No one can see Sensei if he does not want them to. Not even we can find him when he chooses to hide from our constant questions."

The man laughs, and the tension releases its fingers from our necks. "The deeds of Ki-Yaga are famous. I have heard he can walk through walls and disappear into the night. But I see he has worked even greater magic. He has taught his students honor *and* good manners. Unlike some others, constantly ringing their bell."

That sounds just like the Dragon Master and his students.

Bowing, the attendant takes his leave. The slap of silk against the floor tracks his departure. Sensei says the Emperor is afraid of assassins. He wants to ensure he can hear everyone coming and going. Especially those on their way across his nightingale floor.

Tap-tap. Tap.

Nezume opens the door cautiously, hoping it's not the Dragon Master.

It is another attendant, older and taller but with the same baggy trousers.

"I have a message for Ki-Yaga, sensei of the Cockroach Ryu," he says, eyes round and respectful. Our teacher is a living legend, the most famous samurai to still have his head on his shoulders. At least for now.

The attendant hesitates. It's not good news. But Sensei smiles encouragingly.

"The M-m-aster of the D-d-d-ragon Ryu sends you a greeting," the attendant stutters. He stares at the bamboo matting. He looks at his slippers, and he even stares at my one foot.

"Please continue," says Sensei. "I will not hold you accountable for another's rude words."

We know the message anyway. *Beware the Dragon.*

The attendant swallows loudly, but he speaks in an embarrassed whisper. "How many cockroach wings can a dragon's breath singe?"

It is a great insolence for the Dragon to threaten a man under the Emperor's roof. But Sensei is not insulted. His eyes gleam.

"The Dragon Master is finally wise enough to consult the bugs."

My eyes twinkle, too. This is a traditional saying that Grandfather uses all the time. If you need to know something, ask the bugs. Bugs can sense shifts in the world around them and predict what might happen next.

This Cockroach predicts that Sensei will wield his words like a sword and cut the Dragon's ears to kite ribbons.

"Tell the Dragon Master that I do not have time to teach him to count. I suggest he use his fingers and toes," Sensei says.

The attendant leaves, grinning. We bathe quickly and eat breakfast even faster. The Owl Ninja truly are excellent cooks.

"Will the Emperor still want to punish you, Sensei?" Kyoko is worried.

"Only when I least expect it," says Ki-Yaga.

"Are you expecting it today?" I ask.

Sensei picks a rice grain from his teeth. "No, I am not."

Now we're all nervous.

Tap-tap. Another knock.

"The Emperor is ready to see you," the attendant announces.

Sensei teaches us that seeing is not important. You must feel. It is too late when you see an army approaching, but if you feel the ground shake, you will expect them before they arrive. You will have the advantage and be prepared.

"You must learn to be like Taji," our master says. "Taji is not distracted by what he can't see."

Wiping his hands on his beard, Sensei is ready to go. But the *ronin* is still eating.

"Aren't you coming?" Yoshi asks him.

"I'll wait here," he answers. "I have no interest in bowing to the Emperor with my stomach only half full. I am loyal to my teacher and will come running when he needs me. But he does not need me now."

Yoshi would like to stay and help him eat but Sensei hurries us along. "Chop, chop, Little Cockroaches."

It's tricky to hop in long, trailing trousers. The Emperor will have no trouble hearing me approach; I'll probably trip at his feet. Two soldiers escort us into the waiting alcove. The Dragon Master is already there. His cloak gleams with gold embroidery, and his helmet is plumed with owl and crane feathers.

We wait in opposite corners, gazes slicing across the room like sword swipes in a battle.

"Someone should stuff an explosive inside his helmet," Mikko whispers.

Grinning, I remember the hole in the Owl Dojo wall. But Sensei doesn't think it's funny. He shakes his head to remind us of our manners.

Two Dragon kids stand beside their master. We recognize the largest boy. He purposely broke Kyoko's hand at the Games last year.

"I'd like to break *his* fingers," Yoshi mumbles through clenched teeth. He could do it, too. He's bigger and stronger than the Dragon boy.

Mikko is small, but his one hand is very powerful. "Let me," he mutters. Mikko could crush even Yoshi's fingers if he wanted to.

"No," counsels Sensei. "It is not an eye for an eye and a hand for a hand."

Nezume fidgets nervously. "Why must we wait so long?"

"The Emperor will be consulting his advisers to make

sure this is a lucky day for making important decisions," Sensei says.

How can a day be lucky? If it's lucky for us, it's not lucky at all for the Dragons.

"His Excellency is ready to receive you," an attendant proclaims.

The two soldiers usher us into a larger room where the Son of Heaven sits on a golden throne, swathed in layers of yellow silk. Biting my lip, I hide my disappointment. The man behind the expensive wrapping doesn't look impressive at all. He is short and round like a rice dumpling, and his fingers are too pudgy even to hold a sword.

Then he smiles.

Sensei is always right. It is not what you see that matters, but what you feel. When the Emperor smiles, the sun reaches down to pat each one of us on the back. The White Crane opens its wings to the warmth.

Grandfather likes to tell stories about the Emperor. "The Son of Heaven makes the crops grow and the rice flourish. But his displeasure can fill the sky with thunder, and when he is angry, lightning shoots from his fingers."

He wouldn't need to hold a sword, then. Maybe he's a ninja.

But in the final battle, great power cannot overcome great fear. Good-luck charms hang from vantage points all over the room. Beside the throne candles burn. Only a brave ghost would dare set foot in this room filled with talismans to keep the spirits away.

Removing his helmet with a flourish, the Dragon Master bows.

"Welcome," the Emperor says.

When Sensei bows, it is a simple gesture of great respect, like rice stalks bending in the breeze.

The Emperor stands. "Teacher," he murmurs, kneeling to touch his forehead against Sensei's feet.

"I would like to introduce my newest students," says Ki-Yaga.

We stand tall and proud. The Emperor is puzzled by what he sees. A one-legged boy leaning between a one-armed boy and a bigger, broad-shouldered one. A white-haired girl holding the hand of a blind boy. Another boy nervously watching the door.

"Are these the students who won the Samurai Trainee Games?" he asks.

"Welcome," the Emperor says.

Sensei nods.

"Cheats," a Dragon kid hisses.

The Son of Heaven is not as wise as Sensei, but he is not foolish.

"I see you have chosen *your* students carefully, Ki-Yaga. You always did." He bows to us. "It is a great honor to share your teacher.

"As you know," he says, resuming the throne, "the Shogun requires me to adjudicate on local matters such as those you bring to the castle court today. You may present your claims. Who will speak first?"

Sensei doesn't move, but the Dragon Master pushes forward. We remember what our teacher has taught us. The slow swordsman needs to go first, to get a head start. A duel of words has begun, and the Dragon Master is behind already.

His voice booms. "I bring a request from both the Lord of the South Mountains and the Lord of the North Mountains. They cordially remind the Son of Heaven that it was his father who sanctioned the Shogun's grant of their daimyo lands. They ask to be allowed to fight their own battles. To wage their own war."

"You have this in writing?" The Emperor leans forward.

Nodding, the Dragon doesn't even try to hide his smirk. He thinks he has won. But Sensei has not opened his mouth yet, and his wisdom can cut through ten rolls of matting.

"I have it here, tucked in my belt."

When the Dragon Master moves to open the scroll, the Emperor raises his hand. "I will hear Ki-Yaga speak now."

The Dragon puffs and blows, but Sensei's voice breathes gently. "I ask the Emperor to intercede and stop this war before death strips the mountains. I do not bring a scroll. I keep my words where all important things belong, between my heart and my sword."

"Does anyone else wish to speak before I make my decision?" The Emperor's gaze includes us, and Yoshi steps forward.

"I would like to ask the Dragon Master a question. Why would any master want his students to fight?"

The Dragon's chest bloats with pride and the opportunity to teach Ki-Yaga's Cockroaches a lesson.

"Because *my* students will emerge victorious and win great honor."

Nezume shakes his head. "They will be covered in blood."

"Or even worse," Sensei says, "they will be covered in cloth."

Dead.

BONG.

A gong sounds and the Emperor rises. "I have other business to attend to. I will think upon your requests and view the scroll in the morning."

BONG. Another gong sounds to dismiss us. The Dragon Master shoves past with a swish of red and gold. But Ki-Yaga waits.

"I have a gift from Sword Master Onaku." Sensei takes a package from under his robe, offering it to the Emperor.

Short, fat fingers grip the hilt perfectly. The sword sings, a song fit for its king.

"Not even an Emperor's riches can pay for a weapon like this," the Son of Heaven says as he caresses the hilt. "Tell Onaku his gift is gratefully accepted. Perhaps your students would like to spend some time with my son in the Imperial Water Garden?"

The Dragon kids aren't invited!

We know the way. We saw the water lilies from the window in our room.

"I'll meet you there." Taji winks. He's going off on his own to listen in and spy out information.

But before he can leave, the Emperor's scream cuts through our plans. His face whiter than Kyoko's hair, the Emperor points to where the three candles closest to the throne are no longer alight. Four still burn, but this is the worst number of all, a disastrous omen. The Emperor collapses on his throne.

Quickly, Sensei moves to relight the candles. "It is only a warning," our master says. "You have been given the opportunity to prevent many deaths."

Sensei waves us away and we're glad to go, eager to play in the garden. The Emperor is in good hands. Sensei is a renowned healer who can set broken pieces of both body and mind.

The Imperial Water Garden is huge, with an enormous pond covered in pink and white flowers. In the middle of the pond is an island, and standing at the water's edge is a boy about our age.

We hurry across the wooden bridge.

"I am pleased to meet you," the prince says. "I hear you wiped the tatami mats with the Dragon Ryu at the Samurai Trainee Games. I wish I'd seen that."

He smiles. The Grandson of Heaven commands the sun, too. I already like this boy a lot. Kicking off our sandals, we sit at the water's edge, letting the koi nibble our feet. It's peaceful here. Our *ryu* garden is full of cabbages, chickens, and stones. There's nothing restful about hard work and calloused hands.

"I am learning swordsmanship, too," the prince says.

Mikko grins. "We could have a practice match. Just for fun."

"I don't know," the prince says hesitantly. "It wouldn't be fair to fight a one-armed opponent."

"You could tie up one hand," Mikko suggests. "What about a wager? If I win, you owe me a gold piece."

The prince wouldn't stand a chance, even with both hands.

"Don't believe him. It's a trick," says Kyoko, glaring

at Mikko. "He could win with no hands and the sword between his teeth."

"Sorry," Mikko apologizes. "But there's a girl I like, and I need to bring her a belt full of money."

The prince winks. "I understand that."

I'm not sure I like the way the prince looks at Kyoko when he says it. Before I can pull my thoughts together, Yoshi changes the subject.

"We came through Hell Valley on our way here, and a ghost spoke to Niya. Sensei says you know a lot about the spirit world."

Trust Yoshi to know what the prince is interested in. Sensei would be pleased. A good samurai is always prepared.

"I wish I could go into the valley. Father says it's too dangerous. He is afraid, but I am not." The prince's eyes shine with excitement. "I've spent years studying but have never seen anything. Ghosts, goblins, shapeshifters, *tengu* . . ."

Mikko pokes me in the ribs, and my friends erupt in giggles.

"Supernatural beings should not be laughed at," the prince says. "Even my father cannot dictate to the other world. Emperor and subjects bow fearfully before the spirits."

"Three candles went out in the throne room," I say. "Your father was very upset."

The prince is not surprised. "When he was a boy, my father was visited by a fearsome goblin—a *tengu* priest from the mountains. The stories that priest told still give my father nightmares, and ever since then, he has slept with two samurai guards at his feet."

"What are the stories?" I ask.

"My father refuses to repeat even one, no matter how many times I plead."

"Niya thinks Sensei is a *tengu* priest," Mikko says, laughing.

The prince doesn't join the laughter. "It's possible," he says thoughtfully. "Some *tengu* are consumed by the darkness, but others give their life to teaching those with a special need."

I like him more than ever. Even if he stares at Kyoko.

"Everyone has goodness and evil in their heart," explains the prince. "We all try to hide the evil so our goodness shines brightest."

Sensei is very good. He could easily outshine a great evil.

"You know a lot about these things," I say admiringly.

"It's not easy being a prince. I don't have any friends, so I read a lot."

It's not easy being us either. But we've always got one another.

The prince pulls a gold coin from his pocket and offers it to Mikko, who shakes his head.

"Take it," the prince insists. "Then you can invite me to the wedding. I am invited many places but never as a friend."

"Thanks. I will." Mikko pockets the coin. "She's the most beautiful girl in all of Japan."

Mikko needs his eyes tested. My sister isn't even a little pretty.

Looking into her reflection, Kyoko sighs deeply. "The Dragon kids say I'm ugly. Who would marry me?"

Someone very lucky, I think.

"I would," volunteers the prince.

I don't like that idea much, but Kyoko is as beautiful as a princess.

Cranky ducks interrupt my thoughts, quacking and

complaining as Taji races across the grass toward the bridge.

"He should slow down. He might trip." The prince looks worried.

Yoshi shakes his head. "Not even if I stick my foot out." He pokes his foot out to prove the point, and Taji skids around it, careening into Nezume.

"I've overheard something really important." He hesitates, unsure whether to trust the prince.

"It's okay. Our new friend has the heart of a Cockroach," says Yoshi.

We never question Yoshi's judgment, except when he's deciding who gets the leftover serving of pudding. But this time it's got nothing to do with dessert.

"The Dragon Master's scroll will be stolen tonight," Taji confides. "While the master and his students are completing their evening exercises, the kitchen boy will deliver their meal and steal the scroll. Without it, the Dragon Master can't prove whom he speaks for."

But Sensei can. He always speaks for himself.

We wish we could tell the prince about the ninja in his kitchen, but it's not our secret to spill, and we promised the Owl Master we would keep it safe.

"Sensei is coming now," announces Taji.

The prince looks at me as Sensei rounds a corner. I shrug. I don't know how Taji does it either.

"Master," the prince stands and bows.

"Grandson of Heaven." Sensei returns the bow. "I have come to meditate in your garden. I hear you have many wise old cherry trees."

"It would be an honor for you to rest beneath their branches," says the prince.

Sensei looks tired. And he looks sad. Perhaps it took all his strength to calm the Emperor's fears. Or maybe he is worried about tomorrow. I hop with him to the oldest, wisest cherry tree, waiting while he settles back against its trunk.

"Are you sad, Sensei?"

He sighs. "I have lived a long time. Longer than any man should."

Are you a man? I want to ask.

"When you have lived as long as I have, you gather many memories. And some are very sad," Sensei says. "Some, I would even give my left leg to change."

Understanding, I nod. I have many happy memories,

and I would not trade a single one of them. Not even for another leg.

"Niya," Kyoko calls, "come and feed the koi."

The moment snaps like a frayed piece of bamboo. Sensei closes his eyes.

"Rest well, Master," I whisper.

Sensei snores. And inside my head, he smiles.

CHAPTER TWELVE

義

IF THE
SLIPPER FITS

Bash. Bash. BASH.

No gentle tap this time. The pounding demands that we open the door right away, before the rice paper rips. Even Yoshi stops mid-breakfast, rushing to answer the knock.

The attendant has run all the way to deliver this message and is gasping for breath. "The Emperor requires an audience with Ki-Yaga." Words tumble and drop so fast that my ears struggle to catch them. "Immediately."

It's not a request. It's a command.

"Chop, chop, Little Cockroaches." Wiping a stray noodle from his beard, Sensei heads out the door. We don't even stop to change into our castle finery. This time the *ronin* comes, too, pausing for one last mouthful and to tuck his wooden sword into his belt.

"What do you need that for?" Mikko asks.

"A stout piece of wood is always useful. Perhaps I will wave it around to make a point."

The point of a wooden sword is rounded and blunt, but even a floorboard would be a convincing weapon in the *ronin*'s giant hands. He might not have the skill and grace of a swordsman, but he has the strength of a huge bear.

Sensei strides along beside the attendant, whistling, the way he does when he's looking forward to something. But I know it's not good news. Good news is more polite. It waits until after breakfast.

Loud and angry, the Dragon Master's voice gusts along the corridor to buffet our ears. Nezume moves closer to Sensei. Our master is not afraid. "The castle's heating is working well this morning. The hallway is full of hot air," he says with a chuckle.

The Emperor's voice rises to quell the Dragon's fire. "I will wait to hear what Ki-Yaga has to say."

When Sensei steps through the doorway, the hush falls like a noose around us. The Dragon Master and his students are standing before the throne. Turning, the Dragon's glare swipes razor-sharp across the room. But our teacher bows effortlessly beneath it.

"How may I be of service?" Sensei asks the Emperor.

"You've caused enough trouble." The Dragon Master has forgotten his court manners, raking a long red finger-nail just beneath Sensei's chin. "You took my scroll."

Sensei shrugs. "I have not seen it. But like the Emperor, I was hoping to check its authenticity this morning."

"You can't trick me this time." The Dragon Master smirks. "I've got proof."

He turns to the Emperor. "When I finished my exercises, our evening meal was on the table but the scroll in the adjoining room was gone. There was only one person who came into our rooms. The castle kitchen boy stole it for *him*." The red nail stabs at Sensei's chest, and the Dragon boys snicker. "Who else but Ki-Yaga would benefit from such a crime?"

Sensei nods. "It is true I have often benefited from the Dragon Master's shortcomings. But should I be held responsible whenever he cannot remember where he has left something?"

The prince is sitting beside his father, and he struggles not to laugh. "Is the Dragon Master suggesting that *our* castle kitchen staff does Ki-Yaga's bidding?" he asks.

Sensei shakes his head, amazed. "Next the Dragon Master will be suggesting the kitchen is full of ninja."

"Ridiculous," the Emperor agrees. "My staff is loyal to me. They are not criminals for hire."

"I can prove it was the kitchen boy. I didn't see his

face, as I was concentrating on an extremely difficult exercise. The foolish culprit was in such a hurry that he left something behind in the scroll's room." The Dragon Master places a slipper on the table. "Call the boy who served me last night and we'll see if the slipper fits."

My heart drops onto my foot so hard I want to hop in pain. I recognize the slipper. It belongs to Ako. He can run like wind across rice, but he'll never outrace the Dragon Master's revenge.

The Emperor reaches for his bell.

Fear spreads like ice through my stomach, but in my memory the ghost's red eyes burn lava-hot. Remembering its words, relief thaws me. *I need only one slipper.* Sensei nods, and the White Crane winks back.

"It is not necessary to find the boy," Sensei says. "I have a confession to make."

"I knew it," the Dragon Master gloats.

"It will be best if Niya explains."

I hop forward. Face flushed, I feel the Dragons breathing hot down my neck. But the White Crane stands still and regal, its one foot firmly anchored in the cool waters of the lake.

"Son of Heaven." I bow. "I must apologize. I am the

one who has caused the Dragon Master to wrongfully accuse your staff and our teacher."

Slowly and respectfully, I bend toward the throne.

"Please continue." Shining like the sun, the Emperor's warm voice gives me even greater courage. What I must say isn't easy for me. Sometimes a samurai kid must use a ninja trick to deceive.

"I was the one who served the Dragon Master's meal. There was no kitchen boy in his rooms, only me. But I didn't go into the room containing the scroll."

The prince smiles encouragingly, but the Dragons have faces like thunder. I close my ears to their rumble.

"I swapped with the kitchen boy because Sensei teaches us that a samurai must be good with a sword on the battlefield and a knife in the kitchen. He is always telling us we need more practice."

"Is this true?" The Emperor knows our master cannot lie to the Son of Heaven.

But Sensei is as clever with words as he is with his sword. He can dodge a question as easily as he ducks under a swinging blade. "Yes. I am always yelling 'More practice.' My students complain about it all the time."

Only the Dragon Master is not convinced. "The Cockroach boy is lying."

"Perhaps someone else entered your room," suggests the Emperor.

"No. I felt only one person enter. I am a Zen master, and I would know if someone else sneaked in. Not even a ninja can creep past me. It is the boy's slipper. Make him try it on. It will prove he was in the scroll's room."

"I would be glad to," I say. "But I cannot. It is for the left foot and I only have a right one. Maybe one of the Dragon students left it there. Perhaps they forget where they leave things, too."

The Dragon Master scowls, and the Dragon kids glare. If looks could kill, I'd be dead many times over by now.

The prince tries not to laugh. But this time he can't help it. Laughter is like a river. It runs from face to face, tickling and teasing. The *ronin*'s voice rumbles. Yoshi roars. Mikko giggles. Even the Emperor smiles.

Slowly, he rises to speak. "I have made my decision."

Kyoko reaches for my hand while Nezume fidgets nervously. Will the Emperor's words silence the drum?

"In battle, when one side loses its scroll of orders, it surrenders. And the other side wins. The theft of a scroll is an ancient and honorable military strategy. And while this does not excuse the culprit from punishment if he is caught, in this case, he is too clever for that."

Inside my head, the drumming finally stops.

But the Dragon is not willing to surrender. He has no respect for tradition or honor.

"Everyone in the castle must try the slipper on," he demands.

Sensei pokes a skinny crow foot forward. "Perhaps it might fit me."

"It is not necessary. The Dragon Master has testified that only the boy who delivered the evening meal was in the room and clearly the slipper is not his," says the Emperor.

"It's another trick," fumes the Dragon. "Ki-Yaga is a black magician. You," he hisses at me, "are just like your master."

There's no greater compliment. "Thank you." I bow.

"War is a game with many rules," Sensei says. "Strategy is always an honorable move. Remember the great warrior who left his opponent waiting while he slept late and ate a leisurely breakfast?"

Our stomachs rumble, remembering the missed meal.

"This young warrior finally arrived, barefoot and half-dressed, carrying only a wooden sword. His enraged opponent slashed wildly, lured into carelessness. The young upstart had won the first of many famous battles."

Everyone knows the story about Mitsuka Manuyoto, but the *ronin* is grinning so wide, it's obvious that Sensei is talking about him. It seems there's more to our big friend's craftiness than simply taking off his trousers. And now we know his name. I was right all along.

The Emperor smiles, welcoming the defender of his youth. But the Dragon Master still doesn't know. He's too angry to listen properly. And he hasn't learned the lesson. His face furrows with fury. "It was a pathetic win. He didn't even kill his opponent. The fool let him escape."

"He wisely chose to let him live," Sensei says. "The greatest victory is always the one with the least bloodshed."

"Is that what you think?" The Dragon Master unsheathes his sword.

The blade flashes only inches from Sensei's long beaked nose.

Behind me I hear the Emperor's guards move, but the Son of Heaven raises his hand to stay them. The war is not over after all, and it is only right for two masters to settle their differences with a blade. Except Sensei hasn't brought his sword with him.

The drumming begins again inside my head. Louder, faster. *THUMP. THUMP. THUMP.*

Sensei doesn't move. He's not in a hurry. Only the slow man needs a head start.

The *ronin's* strong voice fills the room as he places his huge body between Sensei and the fire-breathing Dragon. "No one insults my teacher. I accept the challenge on his behalf."

"You? I'm not fighting a beggar," the Dragon bellows. There's no glory in slicing the head from a street tramp, but the man who collects Sensei's head will have many stories told about him.

But it's not up to the Dragon Master. Ki-Yaga's voice rings with even greater authority than the gong. "I accept my student's offer."

Our teacher waves us to the back of the room, where

the castle guards are standing, hands on their swords. The Dragon kids move, too, staying as far away from us as possible. Only Sensei, the *ronin,* and the Dragon Master remain in front of the throne.

"Cockroaches smell," the big Dragon boy mutters.

Kyoko pokes out her tongue. "And Dragons stink."

Phew. Mikko and Taji pinch their noses shut.

"Shh," Yoshi says.

"This filthy *ronin* doesn't even have a proper sword," the Dragon Master sneers.

I smile, and Yoshi chuckles softly.

A true samurai doesn't need a sword.

"I have all I need." Grinning, the *ronin* pulls the wooden *bokken* from his belt.

The Dragon's mouth curls in contempt. "It's just a practice sword."

"Not in my hands. And anyway, I am only intending to practice on you. Maybe tomorrow I will find a worthy opponent."

If the Dragon Master really could breathe fire, the room would be filled with smoke and ash. Instead, it is choked with rage and anger.

"I will not fight against street trash." He folds his

gold sleeves across his chest.

"All that glitters is not gold," Nezume whispers.

"Sometimes it is just shiny rubbish." Kyoko giggles.

Sensei is a great teacher, and the *ronin* was his greatest pupil. It's not over yet.

"It appears that the Dragon is too timid to fight me." The *ronin* waits, hands on his hips.

"I'll fight," sneers the Dragon Master. "But you'll regret your words when I chop your sword into firewood."

"As my student is fighting on my behalf, may I provide him with a sword?" Sensei asks the Emperor.

The Son of Heaven nods.

Sensei pulls a cloth bundle from under his cloak, then unwraps the extra sword Onaku gave him.

The *ronin* reaches for it, eyes bright as he recognizes the Sword Master's handiwork. From here I can see that the grip is unusual. It melts into the *ronin*'s hand, and as flesh and sword join together, I hear the blade sing. Everyone can. It drowns out the thump of the drum.

"Onaku knows how to make a proper sword." The *ronin* swings the blade in a wide arc, barely missing the gold buttons on the Dragon Master's jacket. Tucking the sword into his sash, the *ronin* stares into the Dragon's eye.

"I am Mitsuka Manuyoto, son of the House of Manuyoto and former student of the Cockroach Ryu. Humble disciple of the great Ki-Yaga. No one insults my master's name unless he wishes to face my drawn sword." Mitsuka doesn't yell his challenge, but his soft words shout in our ears. "I am a Little Cockroach and a destroyer of Dragons. Sheath your sword and apologize. Or fight me."

Mitsuka is a legendary swordsman, but the Dragon is skilled, too. And a cheat.

Can the Dragon cheat enough to win?

"I don't like this," I mutter through gritted teeth.

Yoshi grins. "I think it will be fun."

"What do you mean?" Kyoko whispers, worriedly twisting a stray strand of white hair.

"The Dragon Master has brought only his sword. Mitsuka has his blade and his brain. Already Mitsuka has made the Dragon so angry that he won't even look him in the face. How can a swordsman read his opponent's eyes if he doesn't even look?"

The Dragon Master raises his sword.

"It's true," Mikko says. "The Dragon is a fool to fight blind. Only Taji can do that and win."

"And I would not be so foolish as to fight Mitsuka Manuyoto," Taji adds.

The Dragon Master raises his sword. Mitsuka watches, waiting until the last moment.

"Stop," the Emperor commands, rising from his throne. "I do not wish to watch anyone die. There will be no fight in this room, just as there will be no war in my mountains." He claps his hands, and an attendant appears. The sound of two hands clapping is loud and powerful when they are the Emperor's hands.

"Place a message in the receptacle at the castle keep gate so a runner can collect it and take my decision to the mountain daimyos. The war drum must cease," the Emperor tells his attendant. "And this foolishness must never happen again. As a measure of their loyalty, the daimyos will send their children to me. And as a measure of my esteem, I will ensure that these children receive the best training my court has to offer. Each of the daimyos has a son, and my own son has no companions. It is a perfect solution."

Yesterday the prince made six new friends and today

promises even more. The Emperor's fingers might be fat and clumsy, but there's nothing pudgy about his brain. The lords will do as they're told while their sons are away. And their sons will be happy here. No one dies, and everyone wins.

Except the Dragon Master. But he hasn't given up yet. One of the Dragon boys bows to excuse himself and leaves.

"I bet two servings of pudding there won't be any message for the runner to find," whispers Mikko.

But we know it doesn't matter. The message has already been received. There are eyes and ears all over the castle, especially in the kitchen. And they all have a ninja runner's legs.

"Instead of a duel, let us now have a friendly display of swordsmanship," the Emperor suggests.

"Two of my students are the best in all the mountains," Sensei says.

Nezume and Mikko step forward. The Dragon kids haven't even moved. Remembering the Games, they don't want to challenge us.

The Emperor is surprised. "How can a great swordfighter have only one arm?" he asks.

"Don't be fooled, Father," the prince says. "I've heard that Mikko can fight with a sword in his teeth. And yesterday he dueled against me for a gold coin without even unsheathing his blade."

"Yes, I remember that lesson well. The true samurai doesn't need a sword," the Emperor says, looking at Ki-Yaga.

Sensei bows. "The Son of Heaven was always a credit to his teacher."

"Perhaps one young Cockroach could fight a Dragon?" the Emperor suggests diplomatically.

"It would be a waste of our skill," the Dragon Master says, bowing to the Emperor but sneering at us. "We do not waste time stomping on bugs."

That's because their clumsy Dragon feet would never catch us.

Placing one hand behind his back, Nezume stares into Mikko's eyes. Cockroaches fight with honor. They wait for Sensei's instruction.

"Draw," he calls.

Two swords flash in the sunlight of the Emperor's approving smile. Long arcs of steel swish. Clash. And move apart again. It's a dance. Lizard scurry. Rat scuffle.

Until Nezume's sword point rests on Mikko's chest.

The prince claps and cheers.

"Looks like I need . . ." Mikko waits for us to finish his sentence.

"More practice!" we yell together.

Next Mitsuka steps forward. Famous for his double swordplay, he swings the *bokken* with one hand and Onaku's sword with the other.

"I am impressed," the Emperor says. "My son is also a keen student of swordplay. Now he will demonstrate the techniques he has learned."

It's a solo display. It wouldn't be appropriate to draw a sword against the prince in front of the Emperor. We're not playing in the garden now.

The prince walks to the middle of the floor and draws his sword in a slow, fluid half circle. He strikes, then flicks it to his other hand.

"Not bad," Mikko murmurs. "There goes my advantage. Maybe I was lucky he didn't fight me."

But the prince hasn't had the benefit of Sensei's teaching. Many of his moves are clumsy and unfinished.

"See how skilled my boy is," the Emperor says, beaming.

"The prince is an excellent swordsman," the Dragon Master says.

"And how would you grade him?" the Emperor asks Sensei.

Sensei is a samurai of the oldest ways. Honor before one's own life. And it's one of those times now.

A sharp sword hangs over Sensei's head.

But our teacher's voice is strong and pure. Like Onaku's steel. "Your son is poorly trained."

Fearful, we wait for the sword to drop and slice the silence.

When the Emperor smiles, we breathe a sigh of relief. There's no sword after all. But we should know better than that. Just because we can't see the blade doesn't mean it's not there.

"In that case, you will stay here and teach him," the Emperor commands.

In our hearts, the sword drops with a clatter.

CHAPTER THIRTEEN

礼

THE SECOND
SCROLL

The Dragon Master laughs. And laughs. There's nothing we can do. Even Sensei can't fight his way out of this one. We wait, hoping he will raise his arms and defiantly shout, *"Banzai!"* Then the room will shake with the power of his *ki,* as it did at the Owl Dojo.

But Sensei respectfully bows his head. "As the Emperor wishes."

The Son of Heaven's smile isn't warm anymore. It burns, and the White Crane cringes.

"Father . . ." the prince starts to speak.

But even a son cannot argue with the Emperor.

"You must say good-bye to your teacher," the Emperor commands us. "Tomorrow morning you will leave with Mitsuka. I am sure Ki-Yaga will agree that you are in good hands."

Sensei nods, holding out his staff to me. I reach into his thoughts, desperate for him to say some words of comfort.

I don't understand, I wail soundlessly.

Sensei smiles. *You must read between the lines.*

But there is nothing there.

He nods, pleased. *Yes. I knew you would understand.*

I understand Nothing. But even Zen can't help me this time.

The room is filled with the loud silence that sometimes falls between cicada songs. No one moves. No one speaks. The White Crane listens hard, but Sensei is not talking anymore. Not even inside my head.

When the Emperor rings his bell, another guard appears. "Take Ki-Yaga to the yellow room and make sure he has everything he requires."

"Is he a prisoner?" the guard asks.

The Emperor shakes his head. "There is no need to secure the door." He knows Sensei's honor is a stronger lock than any piece of metal.

"You may go now." With a dismissive wave, we are separated from our teacher. It hurts. More than the thump of the war drum against my chest. More than the time I was caught in a mudslide and couldn't breathe.

Turning, I catch the look of helplessness on the prince's face. The Dragon Master grins triumphantly. His students smirk, twisting their fingers into half-hidden rude gestures.

"Ha!" the largest Dragon boy mouths at us.

Little Cockroaches have no heart for slaying Dragons now. Even Mikko doesn't retort. Our feet drag, numb like our spirits. The White Crane huddles, curled in a tight ball.

Outside in the corridor, Kyoko bursts into tears.

"What will we do?" Mikko's voice shakes.

"Should we go home?" asks Nezume.

Even Yoshi has no answers. Suddenly, we are all children, looking to Mitsuka for help.

Our *ronin* shrugs, unconcerned. "You do not need me to tell you what to do. I am not the one holding Sensei's staff."

All eyes turn to me.

"But Yoshi is our leader," I protest, pushing the staff into his hands.

"That's true, but"—he waves it away—"you are our teacher now."

I can't be. I know nothing.

Perfect, Sensei whispers.

I reach out, clutching for more advice. But it's one last whisper and he's gone. I've always wanted to be a teacher, but I'm not ready. I am still just me. Niya.

Then I understand. I am the White Crane. Brother of the Tiger, the Golden Bat, the Striped Gecko, the Snow Monkey, the Long-Tailed Rat, and the Great Bear. Friend and ally of the Owls. I am not alone.

"Don't worry. Together we'll work something out," I promise. "But we can't talk here. The castle is full of ears, and I bet the corridor is lined with listeners."

I hop ahead in a hurry. The others rush to keep up.

"He thinks he really is Sensei now," Mikko puffs beside me.

"Chop, chop, Little Cockroaches," I say, teasing.

At the door to our room, Riaze is waiting, morning tea tray in hand. He already knows about Sensei. And he also knows we didn't finish breakfast.

"I've come to help," he offers.

"Thank you." I bow, and Kyoko gives Riaze a big hug.

"Go and check that no one is spying," Yoshi instructs Taji. "Make sure all the doors and windows are slid shut," he tells Nezume and Mikko.

Taji takes the ninja listening cup from under his kimono and places it in turn against each of the four walls. Mikko rushes around checking windows, and Nezume ensures that the door latches are pulled tight.

The Cockroach Ryu is a family. My friends would give me the slippers off their feet. But you can't trust just anyone you meet in the castle — anyone outside of the kitchen, anyway.

Sensei isn't talking inside my head, but that doesn't matter. All the lessons he ever taught us are stored there. "You must find your opponent's weakness," he instructed us when we struggled to ride Uma.

"What is the Emperor's weakness?" I ask my friends.

"Bad judgment?" queries Mikko. "He took Sensei away from us."

"No." Yoshi shakes his head. "Keeping Sensei as his son's teacher is a sign of good judgment."

Kyoko sniffs, wiping her nose on her kimono sleeve. "There must be something."

"Are you crying?" I touch her gently on the shoulder.

"Of course I'm not," she says, her voice shaking as she shoves my hand away. "I'm just as brave as you."

I don't feel brave at all. I'd like to tell her that but it wouldn't help either of us. What we need is an idea.

"Remember how the Emperor cowered when

the candles burned out?" Nezume asks. "He is very superstitious."

"That's it! The prince said the Emperor is terrified of *tengu* most of all," I exclaim.

Jumping and hopping, we slap each other on the back, celebrating our cleverness and Sensei's imminent return.

But Mitsuka stands apart with an amused smile on his face. "All you need to do now is find a *tengu.*"

Defeated, Kyoko flops onto the floor. "It's a terrible plan. We'll never get Sensei back."

"Sometimes students must think hard to remember their lessons," counsels Mitsuka, helping Kyoko to her feet.

"It's true. Only a blind kid can see what is right under his nose." Taji shakes his head in exasperation at all of us. "What does Sensei say?"

"You don't have to see something to know it's there," we chorus.

"We just have to make the Emperor think it is," Riaze agrees. "Ninja use tricks like that all the time, and a superstitious man is easy to fool."

But Nezume is still unsure. "Is it right to deceive the Emperor?" he asks.

"It's the only way," I insist. "Sensei gave his word. He'll never leave without the Emperor's permission."

Mikko flaps his arms like wings. "I could make a crow noise. *Croak. Croak.*"

"Terrible," we groan.

"You sound like a frog. This is a crow." Kyoko clears her throat. "*Caw, caw.*"

"We could use black ink to dye an owl feather from Sensei's staff," Yoshi suggests.

"And I could use my new ninja skills to make an exploding egg." Mikko waves his arm excitedly. "We can put the feather inside and *poof!* When the smoke clears, the Emperor will see a *tengu* feather. He'll be scared stiff."

Mitsuka's eyes shine with Sensei's familiar twinkle. "How will that make the Emperor release Ki-Yaga?"

"We'll use blood-colored ink to write Ki-Yaga's name on the feather," I say. A name written in red is a bad sign, even on a lucky day. "The Emperor will want Sensei to go as far away as possible."

We're all thinking the same thing. Soon we'll be safely back at the Cockroach Ryu.

"We need to hurry," Riaze says. "The Son of Heaven will be in the library reading now. It's the perfect opportunity. I'll distract the samurai guards while Kyoko uses her new *shuriken* throwing skills to roll Mikko's egg at the Emperor's feet."

We work quickly to put our plan into action. We can't afford to fail. We're not battling for a trophy like at the Samurai Trainee Games. The prize is much more important than that. But the Cockroach Ryu is a powerful team. And we've got an Owl Ninja and a famous swordsman to help us.

The egg lands in exactly the right place. Kyoko caws loudly. We are creeping away when I hear the *pfft* of the explosion as the egg breaks open, delivering our message. I can imagine the Emperor's fear: I wish we didn't have to frighten him. But we're desperate to rescue Sensei.

Time crawls as we wait in our room, listening to the

flurry of the castle responding to its Emperor's cries. Soon the gong will sound and the Emperor will call us into his presence to announce Sensei's release.

We wait for the summons. We wait and wait.

Finally, Mitsuka gets to his feet. "I'll go and see what is happening."

We wait again. But this time it's not for long.

Mitsuka appears in the doorway at the same time as Riaze. Both their faces tell the same story—and it's not good news.

"The Emperor is terrified," Riaze says in a rush. "He believes the time of the *tengu* prophecy from his unrepeatable stories has begun. He wants Sensei by his side to help and advise him."

Our plan has backfired. Who would have thought things could get worse? We huddle together miserably.

"I should have considered what the *tengu* might have said to the Emperor," I mumble.

"It's not your fault." Mikko tries to comfort me. "We all agreed on the plan."

"And next we'll try a new plan," Yoshi says. "Niya will think of something else. He always does."

If only it was that easy. I grip Sensei's staff for support, wishing I could ask his advice. "Yoshi is right. We can't give up. How many times did we compete in the Trainee Games before we were successful? It takes more than one spark to start a fire."

Taji smiles. "That sounds like something Sensei would say."

"I made it up myself," I say, beaming.

As I look at my friends' faces, the room is full of bright sparks. Surely not even the Emperor could stand firm against all our spirits working together.

"Do you remember the scroll in my grandfather's tearoom?" I ask.

Riaze recites:

"The rat scuttles, the big cat creeps, the monkey dashes,
The bat glides, the white crane soars, the lizard darts,
And the owl hoots
In the middle of the night."

"How do *you* know?" Taji asks, amazed. "You weren't even there."

"I helped Niya's grandfather with the calligraphy."

It makes sense now. The fireworks. The long disappearances. And falling asleep at the inn. Not an old man's laziness, but a ninja watching through half-closed eyes. My grandfather is an Owl, too. He knew the time would come when I would need to be reminded of the power of friendship.

"Tonight we'll help the White Crane deliver a new message from the *tengu*. This time we'll frighten the Emperor into releasing Sensei," I say.

Taji grins. "That's excellent. He'll think he's seen a ghost."

In my mind, the White Crane raises its wings in the moonlight and the haunting begins.

"We'll need a way to get past the samurai guards," says Yoshi.

A samurai guarding the Emperor would be a skilled and fearsome foe. The sort of warrior we all hope to be one day.

"I can help." Opening his hands, Riaze reveals a pill in each palm. One brown. One cloudy gray. "Do you want the samurai to doze for the night, or will I send them to sleep forever?"

"No." Nezume shakes his head vigorously.

"We're not going to kill anyone," snaps Kyoko.

Mitsuka growls threateningly.

It's not the samurai way.

"All right. But they'll have sore heads in the morning." Riaze's eyes gleam with pleasure.

We might be friends with the Owl Ninja, but Riaze's words remind me that we will always be different. But Sensei was right, too. The ninja and samurai must work together. And tonight his freedom depends on it.

"We need to find out as much as we can about the Emperor's sleeping arrangements," I say.

We know where to find his head. The dead are buried facing north, so a fearful man always places his pillow pointing south. In our *ryu* bedroom, we are not afraid and our mattresses are bare. "You are not soft in the head, so you do not need pillows," Sensei told us.

"I'll find out who is delivering the evening meal to the Emperor's guards and arrange for a sleeping tablet to be slipped into their *sake*," says Riaze.

"I'll work out the best way to climb up to the Emperor's bedroom," Kyoko volunteers.

"The rest of us will listen in the corridors and compounds," Yoshi says.

And I have a task to complete, too. The White Crane

wants its feathers back. It doesn't like to see them on the Dragon Master's helmet. And Sensei's staff needs a new feather, too.

Mitsuka grins. "It is a good plan. A samurai must be well prepared. Otherwise he will have to resort to surprise tactics and take his trousers off."

"Never," protests Mikko. "We want to frighten the Emperor, not make him laugh."

It makes *us* laugh, though. And laughter binds us together, tighter than a sushi roll.

"It's going to rain tonight," Riaze says.

Ninja always know these things. And it's good news. Clouds will ensure that the night is deep and dark. Thunder and lightning will help us scare the Emperor.

Everything is organized. Even the weather.

A moment later I notice that Riaze has gone. Even in broad daylight a ninja can disappear into thin air.

As the night lengthens, rain smashes against the roof. The wind howls like a wolf facing into the storm.

At exactly midnight, Mitsuka rises, tucking both his *bokken* and his sword into his sash. Yoshi slides the door open. He hoots softly, then listens for Riaze's answer. We slink into the dripping shadows, our ninja-blue uniforms lost in the darkness, wind, and rain.

Phlat.

A large shape drops directly in front of Kyoko, and her scream is sucked into the roaring wind.

"Shh," we chorus.

"It's not my fault," she mutters, glaring into Riaze's barely visible eyes. Then she giggles. "But I wasn't half as loud as the shushing. SHHH." When the Snow Monkey mimics, we can't help laughing.

"It is always good to begin with laughter," Mitsuka says approvingly.

We creep and slosh across the compound until we reach the eastern tower.

Kyoko points. "There's the window to the royal sleeping quarters."

This afternoon Taji counted twelve guards between

the tower door and the Emperor's bedroom. And that was when the Son of Heaven wasn't even there. So tonight we're going over the rooftops to drop in from above.

Quickly, we attach our hand and foot claws. The stacked rock wall of the nearby servants' building is notched with easy handholds, but the blustering rain pushes and shoves against us. We climb single file, sheltering behind the body in front. Yoshi goes first, his broad shoulders bearing the brunt of the storm.

Below us, Mitsuka melts into the shadows, standing watch until we return.

Ptt. Pttt.

Suddenly, Mikko loses his footing and his leg swings free, dislodging a shower of stones. Just behind him, I maneuver my shoulder under his foot. We're all leaning on one another tonight. It makes us strong.

"Thanks," whispers Mikko.

"You better hope you didn't rain rocks onto Mitsuka's head," I say.

Nezume laughs beneath me. "I bet he could parry them with a single sword thrust."

I bet he could slice them into quarters as well.

On top of the roof, I look west to where the ocean rolls beneath the darkness. The wind crashes like waves onto the shore, and the White Crane yearns to fly above the spray. One day, I promise myself. One day we'll go over the sea.

Riaze unloops a rope from his belt.

"Let me do that," volunteers Kyoko.

Expertly, she tosses the rope across the gap between the two towers. *Clunk.* The hooked end claws into stone. Like throwing *shuriken* stars.

Next, Riaze tugs a harness from his bag. "This will ensure that no one falls. We'll cross, one by one, sending the harness back for the next climber."

I know Riaze won't need it. And neither does Kyoko. She brushes it aside, takes hold of the rope, and deftly climbs across. It's easy for a Snow Monkey.

The White Crane can fly, but my foot likes to feel the ground underneath it. It's a long tumble to the courtyard below. I'm not too proud to tie the harness around my waist and inch my way across. My fingers ache, numb against the slippery rope. Rain slaps me in the face, scolding me for my foolishness.

From the main tower roof, it's a short climb down to

the Emperor's window balcony. At the ledge, I remove my claws and drop noiselessly into the Emperor's room. My friends stay on the balcony. The slumbering samurai don't even stir.

There's only one more barrier between me and the Emperor. The nightingale floor.

Taking the flute from her pocket, Kyoko plays a haunting six-fingered tune to hide the sighs and creaks as I creep across the floorboards to the southern end of the Emperor's mattress. We don't want the nightingale's song to call any more guards. We want them to think that the Emperor is listening to a late-night lullaby.

Groaning and turning, the Emperor, with his huge belly, shakes the bed. Gradually, my presence behind him seeps into his dreams. He wakes in fright.

"Guards!" he shouts to his samurai, but they're lost, deep within their ninja-induced nightmares.

Pfflt. Mikko's smoke egg lands on the nightingale floor, perfectly tossed by Kyoko. The smoke rises like an eerie gray fog rolling across the marsh to wrap the White Crane in mist.

I stand still, arms raised high.

Outside, the storm grows, pounding its fists against the roof. The wind batters and bawls.

"Who's there?" the Emperor cries out into the darkness. "Show yourself. I can't see you." His words command, but his voice shakes. "Who are you?"

Only the flute wails in answer, its eerie notes fading as the storm tires.

Into the silence, the White Crane cries, *"Aye-ee-yah."* Four times. Not loud enough to disturb the guards stationed on other floors but harsh enough to scrape like fingernails down a bamboo bucket.

"I am the White Crane, messenger of the black *tengu*." My voice echoes around and around, until it is impossible to tell which direction it came from.

I see shadows move on the balcony as my friends join hands to support me. The room fills with the strength of our *ki*. Pulling the covers over his head, the Emperor huddles into his bedclothes.

"What do you want from me?" the Emperor moans.

"Whoo, whoo," Riaze hoots through the window.

Not what, but who.

"Release Ki-Yaga," the White Crane shrieks. "Now is not the time foretold. But if you continue to ignore the *tengu*'s instruction, greater disaster will strike."

I'm even scaring myself.

"But I need his help." Desperation makes the Emperor bold.

"Is your need greater than mine?"

The Emperor's answer is barely a whimper.

Pfflt. Another smoke egg breaks open, and the fog thickens. The flute cries. Hidden by the fog, Yoshi creeps with ninja steps across the nightingale floor, placing four candles at the foot of the Emperor's mattress. Four flames facing north. As soon as Yoshi is back on the balcony, the White Crane screeches again.

"Did you not see the candles the *tengu* blew out this morning? Can you not see the flames that burn at your feet tonight?"

Sitting up now, the Emperor gasps at the four wisps of light curling through the smoke.

"Let Ki-Yaga go free," the White Crane shrieks, even louder than before.

"I w-will," the Emperor stutters.

"Samurai's honor?"

"Samurai's honor," he repeats. It's an oath powerful enough to bind even the Son of Heaven.

I place two white crane feathers and a dyed owl feather on the royal pillow. Tomorrow morning, the Emperor will have a reminder and the Dragon Master's helmet will be bare.

Sensing my movement behind him, the Emperor spins around, peering, frightened, into the fog. Lightning flares, and for an instant, my shadow is caught. The White Crane stands motionless, its wings to the sky.

Pfflt. A third egg rolls into the room.

"Time for us to go," Yoshi calls softly. "Quickly." He reaches to help me out the window.

As I climb through, the moon edges from behind a cloud. This is more dangerous than a stab of lightning; Yoshi and I are about to be caught in a slash of moonlight.

Then, suddenly, a large black shape flies in front of the moon. Perfect timing. Yoshi pulls me to safety so fast that I lose my footing and tumble off the balcony ledge. Luckily, beneath me, Mitsuka steps out of the darkness, arms outstretched. I land with a hammering heart and a soft thump in the Bear's great arms.

Then, suddenly, a large black shape
flies in front of the moon.

We hurry across the compound, then finally pause to catch our breath. Mitsuka's eyes stare beyond me, into the sky. But the shape is gone.

"What was that?" Mikko asks.

"*Tengu*," I murmur.

Mikko laughs. "Don't be silly. *Tengu* don't exist. We were just pretending."

"Before Hell Valley, you didn't believe in ghosts either," Nezume reminds him.

"Maybe it was an owl," Yoshi suggests. But he doesn't look as if he believes his own words.

"It wasn't an owl," Riaze says. A ninja would know.

"It is not our concern," Mitsuka decides.

But it is mine. And one day I'll know the answer. One day I'll ask Sensei my question.

The White Crane ruffles its feathers, rain dripping in puddles at its feet. The Tiger shakes its soggy fur. We're wet, cold, and bedraggled, but we're proud. And Sensei would be, too.

Before we reach our room, Riaze stops. "It's time for me to leave. Good-bye, Little Cockroaches. You have owl wings now."

"You are a friend truly worthy of Izuru," I say, bowing deep.

"We will never forget you," promises Kyoko.

"Until we meet again," Riaze says, and kisses her hand.

He bows to Mitsuka. Then to all of us. One blink and he's gone, faded into the shadows.

Behind me Taji hoots softly. And all along the castle wall, owls echo the Golden Bat's call.

CHAPTER FOURTEEN

勇

FLIGHT OF
THE CRANE

BONG. BONG.

The castle gong rings loud and insistent. We don't care about our interrupted breakfast this time. We race Mitsuka through the garden and along the corridor to spill, breathless, into the Emperor's presence. This morning there are even more charms and candles in the room.

"I have had a dream," he announces. "I have received a new message from the black *tengu*. Ki-Yaga must leave the castle immediately or a great disaster will befall the Empire."

The gong sounds again.

The Emperor has spoken, and his word is law.

Kyoko throws her arms around Sensei. We all follow, and soon our teacher is lost beneath a pile of arms and legs.

"My students are powerful in spirit," Sensei says, unpeeling our layers. "And strong in their loyalty." He winces as Yoshi squeezes him tight.

The Dragon Master frowns disapprovingly at our affection. He doesn't understand. His students are in awe of their teacher. But there's no respect in their groveling, only fear. Still, I don't feel sorry for them.

"We all get what we deserve," Sensei once said to us as he handed out heaping bowls of honey rice pudding.

Some kids deserve extra dessert, and some deserve the Dragon Master.

I do feel sorry for the prince. He almost had the best teacher in the world.

Sensei bows low to the Emperor. "You are both wise and generous. But now the Grandson of Heaven has no tutor to improve his swordsmanship. Allow me to provide him with one of my students."

My mouth drops open. I don't want to stay here.

But it's not me. Nezume has already moved to stand before the Emperor.

"It's a ridiculous suggestion." Pushing his way forward, the Dragon Master knocks against Nezume. This time, our Long-Tailed Rat doesn't cringe. Staring into the Dragon's eye, he stands firm.

"The boy belongs to me," the Dragon Master exclaims, simmering with barely controlled rage. "His father sent him to the Dragon Ryu. He is not Ki-Yaga's to offer or give away."

"Is this true?" the Emperor asks Nezume.

"In the beginning, I was a Dragon boy," Nezume

admits, "but under my first master's guidance, I committed a great wrong. Yet I was forgiven." He bends toward Mikko. "My honor was reborn when I became a Cockroach. My skill as a swordsman grew from my second master's love and care. Today I am proud to be the Emperor's humble servant."

The Son of Heaven smiles. "It would seem that in the end, the boy belongs to me."

Eyes blazing, the Dragon Master bites his lip to hold in the words.

The Emperor has not finished questioning Nezume. "Why should I let you teach my son when *you* are still a student yourself?"

"I am the fastest sword in the mountains. Even Sensei cannot match me."

"Neither can I," admits Mitsuka.

Still, the Emperor is undecided. "I was impressed with your expertise in the demonstration match, but do you have any teaching experience?"

Nezume's voice rings strong and true, like the blade of his sword. "I have never been a teacher, but I have been taught by the best and the worst. I know what a teacher should not do." He lets his jacket slip from his shoulders, revealing a spiderweb of cruel red scars.

The Emperor glares at the Dragon Master. "It seems some *teachers* should be taught a lesson."

Beside me the Bear growls softly, grinding his teeth. "I'd like to do that."

"My service is much more than my sword skills," Nezume continues. "I offer friendship and honest counsel. As you have trusted Ki-Yaga, your son can trust me."

Sensei nods. "All my students are destined for great things. For Nezume, that journey ends here at the castle. This is the task I have trained him for."

"Rubbish," huffs the Dragon Master. "He is just a boy. I should teach the prince."

"I have seen the result of your lessons. You and I will discuss the Dragon Ryu's training methods later," the Emperor says sharply.

I wouldn't want to be standing in the Dragon Master's slippers then. But I'd like to be a cockroach on the wall, listening in.

The Emperor bows to Nezume. "Welcome to your new home, Teacher."

Sensei has sliced another master sword stroke. Now Nezume is safe from the Dragon Master forever. Our friend will grow powerful, whispering in the ear of the future Emperor.

"How can I compensate you for the loss of a student?" the Son of Heaven asks Sensei with a smile. "I recall that we have an outstanding debt to be settled. Perhaps you would like to keep your head."

Yes! We'd all like that.

But Sensei has other priorities. "I do not value my head," he says. "I have a special request."

The Emperor raises his eyebrows. "Then ask."

"It has been decreed illegal to travel outside of Japan. I request a special exemption from the traveling ban. I wish to take my students on a journey over the ocean."

The White Crane stirs, daring to hope. In my imagination it stretches its wings, ready to take flight.

"So be it." The Emperor claps his hands. "Your head is no longer forfeit *and* you are free to leave these shores."

Smirking, the Dragon Master doesn't bother to hide his pleasure. "Finally, I am rid of you." He scowls at Sensei. "A man your age should be dead by now anyway."

The Emperor's stare would slay a lesser Dragon,

but Sensei nods. "Sometimes the Dragon Master is accidentally wise." He strokes his long white beard. "I am always pleasantly surprised to wake up and find I am still alive."

It's probably a good idea for Sensei and the Dragon Master to have an ocean between them.

"Go now, before I change my mind and decide that my son deserves two teachers," the Emperor says. "I must consult my advisers and make an offering to the *tengu*."

Bowing deep and low, we touch our noses to the floor. Our audience is over. The Emperor waves the rest of us away, but he beckons Mitsuka closer.

Halfway back to our room, Sensei stops. A puzzled look on his face, he holds his traveling staff horizontally across his palms.

"Is something wrong, Sensei?" I ask. "I took great care of it. I even added a crane feather to its neck. One I freed from the Dragon Master's helmet."

"The staff is much stronger now that it holds your spirit with mine." The wizard's blue eyes gaze deep into my soul, searching. The White Crane blinks beneath the stare but doesn't look away.

Sensei raps the ground with his staff, and the moment

is broken. "Come along, Little Cockroaches. We have much to do."

We pack slowly, delaying the time when we have to say good-bye to Nezume. But it comes anyway, rushing toward us like a summer monsoon. Nothing will ever be the same once it has passed through our lives.

Kyoko sniffs. "I'll miss you, Rat Boy."

"Don't cry." Nezume wipes her tears with his sleeve. "When Sensei said one of us would stay, I knew it was me. It felt right. I wish I could describe it better."

I understand and I'm good with words, so I help explain. "It's like when I put my foot in my slipper. It fits perfectly."

"Or your mouth." Mikko laughs. "That's a good fit for your foot, too."

Nezume chuckles, and even Kyoko giggles. Mitsuka slides the door open and steps into a room filled with laughter.

"The Emperor has given me a special task," he announces, obviously pleased.

"And what would that be?" Sensei's eyes dance.

I'll bet my second helping of dessert that he already knows.

"The Son of Heaven would like me to teach the Dragon Master a lesson. In the future he will show more care for the welfare of his students." Mitsuka slaps his hand against his scabbard. "It is a task worthy of Onaku's blade."

I wish I could be there, but the way of the warrior has many paths. Not every road leads directly to the ocean. Nezume and Mitsuka will travel their different ways. The Bear will one day return to his cave by the sea while the Long-Tailed Rat scurries the castle corridors.

"I'll walk with you as far as the castle keep gate," Nezume says.

For once Sensei doesn't stride ahead. He shuffles. This is hard for him, too. We walk in silence because truly important moments don't need words to paint their picture. They hang in the mind forever, like an ancient and treasured scroll.

At the castle keep gate, the guards bow deep to Sensei. To Mitsuka. To Nezume, the prince's swordsmanship tutor. And finally to us.

Samurai kids don't like rules. We whine about the tea ceremony and complain about practice schedules. But now we're glad to hide under the formalities of saying

Sensei takes Nezume's hands in
his own and bows.

good-bye. It helps us pretend to be brave. We're not afraid of ghosts or Dragons, but leaving a friend cuts like a ninja dagger; it sneaks up behind, slashing deep.

Sensei takes Nezume's hands in his own and bows.

"*Chi, jin, yu.*" He bows again. "*Meiyo.*"

Wisdom, benevolence, courage.

And honor.

Sensei is proud, and Nezume grows taller beneath his gaze.

The rest of us form a line, ready to offer our own parting words, carefully chosen from Sensei's teaching.

"A true samurai doesn't need a sword," says Yoshi.

We all knew he would say that. It's the first lesson Sensei taught us, and Yoshi's favorite ever since then.

"The point of a sword is very sharp." Mikko prods Nezume in the ribs to remind him.

Kyoko says nothing. Taking her sword from her sash, she slices a twisted thread of snow-white hair and tucks it into Nezume's kimono sleeve.

Taji goes next. "Just because you can't see something doesn't mean it's not there," he says. "We will always be standing beside you."

Even Mitsuka has something to add. "A samurai should be prepared. Otherwise he might lose his trousers."

The Bear can always make us all laugh and, remembering his big hairy legs, we laugh until it brings tears to our eyes. Now I know exactly what to say, too.

"It is always good to begin with laughter."

"But it's not a beginning." Kyoko's tears of laughter drip into sadness. "Our time with Nezume is ending."

We're the only family Kyoko has ever had, and it's hard for her to let a brother go. Six fingers hold tight.

Help her, Sensei says.

"An ending is just another beginning," I say, placing my arm around Kyoko's shaking shoulders.

"That's true," Taji agrees, undoing her fingers from Nezume's hand. "It's all about how you choose to look at things."

And Taji would know. He's always seen things differently, and now he's helping us to look at Nezume with our hearts, not our eyes. Helping us to hang the memory scrolls, so we never forget.

Raising his arm, Sensei signals good-bye. Then he turns, leaving without another word. There's nothing more to say. We hurry after him, but this time Nezume isn't running with us. He stands still, waving. Over and over I look back, until we round the curve in the road and I can't see him anymore.

We thread our way through the maze of streets toward the outer gate. It's not the same without the Long-Tailed Rat scuffling beside me. The others feel it, too. Kyoko's flute wails softly, and in its song, the wind rips the blossoms from the cherry branch. It's left bare. Empty. Incomplete.

"Do not be sad," Sensei says. "We are like seeds blowing in the wind, but Nezume has found the place to plant his roots."

"Sounds like a gardening lesson," I say grumpily.

"Excellent, Niya." Sensei beams at me. "It is how things grow. I am a great lover of trees. And I am always pleased when my seeds sprout roots."

Sensei grows trees all over the *ryu* grounds. Cherry, plum, and oak. But he's not talking about those. He means us.

"Well, now that Nezume is a tree," I tease, "at least we'll always know where to find him."

"Yes," Sensei says, nodding at Mitsuka. "Friends always know where to find each other when they are needed."

We pass through the outer gate and are once again on the Toyozawa road. But Mitsuka is looking in the opposite direction from us. Our *ronin* is leaving, too.

"Don't go," I plead. "Come with us."

He shakes his head. "I have a Dragon to tame. When you return, I will be waiting on the shore, ready to hear your stories and learn the new knowledge my teacher will bring."

"Why would you want to learn anything more?" asks Mikko, amazed.

"There is always one more lesson to be learned, and a teacher is for life," says Mitsuka.

"Life is a very long time." Sensei's eyes smile. "None of my students are ever rid of me."

And I bet they're all as glad as I am.

Mitsuka bows again. "Teacher," he says. Then he envelops Sensei in a giant bear hug.

"Friend," I hear Sensei whisper in reply.

A big bear can move quickly when it wants to, and in no time, Mitsuka is a long way down the road. As I watch, he turns, waving his wooden sword.

"Your students did well in the test you set them,

Master." His voice booms back to us, his laughter chasing behind.

Surely, it wasn't just another test? But then, Sensei never stops teaching.

One day I want to be a teacher. But today has chosen Mitsuka and Nezume, not me.

The time will come, the wizard says. *You will be a great teacher. But first you must learn great things. And you must swim in the sea.*

"Is it far to the ocean?" Kyoko asks.

"Walking quickly, we will reach Japan's edge at sunset," Sensei says.

"Hurrah." Mikko jumps high, kicking his heels together. "If we're not going back to school, we don't have to study anymore. We're on vacation."

Sensei pokes Mikko with his traveling staff. "A school is just a building, but learning is inside you. It follows you around like a shadow."

"And a teacher is forever." Taji pokes Mikko, too. "You'll never get out of school."

"More practice," Yoshi, Kyoko, and I chorus, our voices mimicking Sensei.

Ki-Yaga grins. "There is twice as much to practice now that you have ninja and samurai skills. But this morning, practice must wait. Chop, chop, Little Cockroaches. We must hurry. Before the Emperor changes his mind."

Sensei strides off down the road.

"Are we running away, Sensei?" I ask, finally catching up to him.

"Certainly not." He smiles. "Cockroaches do not run. They scurry with honor and dignity."

And the White Crane flies. With honor and dignity. Sweeping ahead of me, it opens its wings and soars out across the ocean.

THE SEVEN VIRTUES OF BUSHIDO

義 GI   rectitude

勇 YU   courage

仁 JIN   benevolence

礼 REI   respect

真 MAKOTO   honesty

名誉 MEIYO   honor

忠誠 CHUSEI   loyalty

USEFUL WORDS

BANZAI   Japanese battle cry of triumph

BOKKEN   a wooden practice sword, usually shaped like a *katana*

BUSHIDO   the samurai code

CHI, JIN, YU   wisdom, benevolence, and courage

EMPEROR   the dynastic ruler of Japan; however, true power was held by the military

KATANA   long curved sword, traditional weapon of the samurai

MEIYO   honor

RONIN   a wandering samurai who serves no master

RYU   school

SENSEI   teacher

SHAKUHACHI   bamboo flute

SHOGUN   military ruler of Japan

WAKIZASHI   short-pointed dagger, a traditional weapon of the samurai

ZAZEN   the practice of Zen meditation while sitting

ACKNOWLEDGMENTS

To my sons—Jackson, who chops out any boring bits, and Cassidy, who is always full of ideas. To my friend and mentor, Di Bates, whose advice is invaluable. To Bill Condon, Vicki Stanton, Mo Johnson, and Sally Hall—word masters and mistresses all. To Bill Stuart, who shared his reference books and expertise. To my editor, Sue Whiting, whose work is magic. To the super supportive team at Walker Books. Thank you.